NINE
TEN
AGAIN

Stories by
PHIL CONDON

Grateful acknowledgement to the following journals, where some of these stories appeared, in an earlier form and/or under an earlier title:

"Nine Ten Again" in *Shenandoah* 59/1 , "The White Beast" in *The Georgia Review* Vol LI #1, "A Country Voice" in *Prairie Schooner* Vol 67 #1, "A Silver Cloud" in *Confrontation* #60/61, "Dogs and Dogs" in The *Seattle Review* Vol XIX #1, "Leaning" as "Home Crowd" in *The Cimarron Review* #114, "Cakewalk" as "Quicksand" in *The Sewanee Review* Vol CVI #1, "Bridgestone, 1963" as "Garden of the Gods" in *Manoa* 10:1.

Copyright © 2009 by Phil Condon
All Rights Reserved
ISBN: 9781932418330
Elixir Press is a nonprofit organization.

NINE TEN AGAIN

Stories by
PHIL CONDON

For Celeste, always

and for Frank Durham

It's staggeringly beautiful at this hour when everyone seems to be going his own private way. Love and murder, they're still a few hours apart.

Henry Miller

War doesn't begin with the first bombs dropped, it doesn't begin with the terror recounted in the newspapers: it begins in the relationships between people.

Helene Cixous

NINE TEN AGAIN	*3*
THE WHITE BEAST	*25*
A COUNTRY VOICE	*41*
A SILVER CLOUD	*59*
CAKEWALK	*79*
PRESIDENT OF SOMETHING	*97*
LEANING	*115*
BETTER FRIENDS	*131*
DOGS AND DOGS	*145*
BRIDGESTONE, 1963	*167*

NINE TEN AGAIN

NINE TEN AGAIN

The sun was a rose streak too faint to have faith in. Clint Mulane downshifted, pumped the clutch, and downshifted again. Crunching through an icy drift, the truck turned wide from pavement onto gravel. Black letters scrolled across both doors of the cab: *Liston Fuels — Can't Beat Our Heat.* A red warning labeled the back of the white tank behind: *Flammable.* Clint wrestled the wheel straight. The crusty old CB unit under the dash blared static and popped twice. It always sounded like it was about to short out, but it wouldn't break down outright, so Liston insisted they keep using it. His voice crackled through now.

"You't Everton's yet, Clint? He called twice."

"He's the last stop. Like every Friday since we all got left on our own down here."

"Mulane, you're my only route to get slower the longer you drive it. You call in like everybody else or—"

Clint jabbed the off button, notched his cigarette between his thumb and finger, and spun the butt far out the window into a snow bank. Clint had quit on New Year's Day 2000, at least one promise to Ruthie he'd made good on. But he carried his last stale pack on the route to show himself his will, plus it was one more way to stay full in Liston's face. This was only the third or fourth he'd had in the last two years, and like the others, he couldn't finish it. As the truck coasted down toward the low-water bridge over Till Creek, backfires reverberated up and down the hollow.

A black mare sheltered under cedar trees by the creek, her

neck stretching low over three strands of sagging barbed wire. Her white breath rose in slow fog through green branches. Clint stopped and stood by the door of the truck, pissing in snow. He zipped up and walked toward the mare, pulling a half-eaten apple out of his jacket pocket. As she crunched it and snorted, the truck engine dieseled and died. A cold quick breeze ruffled the cedars.

Clint stared straight into the wind, as if he might see where it came from. Beyond the wire fence was the back part of his daddy's old place, the ground Clint grew up on and still ran to in his dreams, good or bad. He took the Till Creek road late every Friday afternoon and called it a shortcut, although it only added time to the route.

The breeze died back. Clint kicked at a patch of snow until he hit frozen gravel. The ground was the same, he thought, despite that another man owned it now. Only the ink on paper had changed, spelling out a new name. It was an old story Clint got tired of hearing and more tired of telling. His daddy fell on hard times. A neighbor climbed up a rung. The American way.

The horse shifted her weight and raised her head, eyeballing Clint. He pulled out another apple from his pocket and gave it to her, rubbing her nose as she ate.

Hunched at his desk in slacks and sports shirt, Buddy Liston signed Clint's check in a flourish of loops and lines. Clint stood across the room. He pulled out a single from the old cigarette pack in his shirt pocket.

"I ever catch you smoking on the route, you're done, Mulane."

"Never happen."

"Me catch you, or you smoke?"

"Either or."

Liston held one hand firm against the payroll book

NINE TEN AGAIN

and tore the check off slowly. Clint heard the perforations crackling one by one, as if each snap counted off a separate hour of his week, his life. Liston stood up, the check in his hand. "You hear what I said?"

Clint walked across the room. He wedged the cigarette behind his ear.

"I came, I saw, I heard. I don't smoke on the route, and you, Mr. 2001 Private Enterprise of Livingston County," he stared at the wall plaque behind Liston, "you, I'll see next month." Beside the plaque hung a wall calendar. The Snap-On Tool Girl, in white pumps and blue bikini, leaned across the open drawer of a bright red mechanic's tool cabinet in her best January pose.

Liston looked back at the calendar, too. "It's Monday, no matter what number, man." He handed Clint the check and flipped the calendar over to February. "You get an off kind of kick out of hating me, don't you, Mulane?" He shook his head. "Here I'm the one writing the checks that fix your froze-up septic, pay your bar bill, and send your kid money, but you can't stand me."

"The septic and my tavern tab both thank you," Clint said as he moved toward the door. "But it would be better if you leave my kid out of it." He caught Liston's eye and held it. "Anyway, what's between you and me isn't hate. You're the boss. You wouldn't want me to like you too much, would you?" He opened the door and stepped out, smiling.

Liston huffed and rolled his tongue over his teeth. "So if it's not me you hate, who would that be then?" The door closed and clicked. "Christ on his tall wooden cross, I pity that man."

⁓

Clint waited in the Friday line at the bank drive-thru, listening to his pickup idle too roughly. The timing was off and the points needed gapping.

He stared at the gray sky beyond town. The route job sucked all week long and only paid up once, but Clint had vowed he wouldn't go back to farm work, except horses maybe, and that wasn't work to him. Damn, if his family wasn't slow-learning. His daddy was a second-generation farmer who rented in town and still worked a Grundy County section the Trenton bank owned most of. Clint wouldn't be a third-generation fool.

He thought of Liston's calendar again and counted back through the long winter weather. Almost six weeks now since Ruthie had packed it in before Christmas and moved to St. Joseph again with the boy. It was nothing Clint would put in a letter, but he missed the hell out of both of them. Maybe he'd give them a call tonight. Ruthie usually put Chase to bed by nine. He'd want to call by then. When Ruthie had left this time, Clint figured he'd just let her fester awhile and sample a few footloose nights again, but it wasn't that easy. The town women didn't party like back whenever. Most of them were married off now, married off and either happy or dangerous. Once in awhile one fell through the cracks, but Clint wasn't the only one looking.

The brick crew down the block at the new Assembly of God church was packing up. They lugged their toolbags and levels out to their pickups. Clint edged up to the window and took his handful of folding money from Annie White, who was as cute as ever, even behind First Federal glass, but married and happy as far as he could see.

∽

Tim Wytter greeted Clint at the door of the Buzz Inn with a Busch and a shot. Missy grilled them two steaks, and by the time Clint's hit the plate with a slap like a hand on a saddle, the Buzz had densed up with a good crowd. Tim talked the usual, his long cold day shooting nails and how they should drive out to the High Hill where there was a

dance floor and lone women.
When they'd both gone liquid enough to head out though, Clint didn't feel up for it. The week bore down on him. Forty hours or forty years, Friday night was a bad time to split hairs. Clint studied the people using the wall phone, making connections, money, time, and it hit him, heavy as a double shot, that Ruthie and Chase were the one family he was ever likely to come by. Clint had always told Ruthie he couldn't live in St. Joseph, not for her or the boy, or the both of them rolled together, which is exactly how they came. In the city, even a small one, it was just too far when you needed to get out in the countryside and watch the weather happen. But then damn near anybody Clint could name had pulled a one-eighty sooner or later when the push shoved hard enough.

"There's no future here," Clint said, louder than he meant to.

"In Marytown?" Tim asked.

"No, New York City, where you think? You know, neither one of us's going to get a second look at thirty again."

Clint had turned thirty-one the month before. This year he got only one card. From his mother. Usually Ruthie would've sent one. Or at least have Chase send one.

"So what's the point?" Tim asked.

"Try Friday nights and Monday mornings. We're watching previews for years, waiting on the show." Clint caught himself and lowered his voice. "Only it don't."

Tim raised his glass and grinned. "To the future then," he said. "Bring on the show."

It was Tim's trademark, wash away whatever comes along with one more brew. Clint shook his head at him but toasted anyway. Tim was a good friend, and like Clint's daddy'd always said, good friends were scarcer than right-hand fingers.

Missy collected their empty plates and brought another round. As Clint reached for the bottle, he hung an eye on Rex

Moorford at the bar, piling up quarters in a little pyramid. The stack of coins summed it all up for Clint. Moorford hadn't worked an honest day in years unless you counted shuffling deeds and gambling on loan points, which Clint didn't. Yet he owned at least four farms clear and paid other men to raise his horses. Ever since he'd bought Clint's daddy out of the homeplace up Till Creek, Clint didn't speak much to him. But if he was anywhere in a room, Clint would know it.

Rex caught Clint's glare. He looked away, but a moment later he walked to their table.

"Tim, Clint. How're you boys doing?"

"Good enough for evening time," Tim said.

Clint pushed his tongue up under his lip and spun his bottle on the table.

"It's a marvel how a man will hear what he hears," Rex said.

"Sit down?" Tim asked Rex but looked at Clint. Clint pointed at the chair like it was up for sale and he didn't care who bought it or at what price. Rex pulled it out and sat down.

"So what might a man hear?" Tim asked.

"Probably nothing important," Rex said. He grinned like he didn't know he woke up every day on the very ground Clint's family had broken. Rex had bought his daddy's half-section for twenty cents on the dollar, but it was still twice what Clint could have paid. "Just small talking and such," he said.

"I always heard said it was little talk for little people," Clint said.

"Okay," Rex said. He spread his hands on the table. "I'll shave her down fine." He smiled at Tim. "If a man wanted himself a real future, I might have just the ticket for him."

"I hope you can hold that thought," Clint said, standing up. He pulled out his cell phone and pointed toward the hallway. He liked throwing Moorford off pace. "I need to make a call."

NINE TEN AGAIN

"They don't make a woman yet who won't wait a little longer," Rex said, half-smiling.

"Nor a king of the tax sales," Clint said.

Tim tipped his bottle up and hid behind it. Clint turned his back and walked, feeling his old grudge hard and sharp, working back to the surface, sure as a splinter.

～

Clint stepped into the hallway where he could hear, dialed the phone, and listened to it ring, trying to remember who told him you can't really tell anything from that toybox sound you hear in your ear, that it didn't mean what everybody thought. Ruthie wasn't home, or didn't answer. He counted up the buzzes anyway.

A stranger came out of the john, combing his hair. His pants were unzipped. Clint was thinking about Labor Day weekend last summer, when Ruthie and Chase were still living with him. The three of them went swimming in the Bighead River. It was one of those picnic days, a Sunday when simple sunlight felt as good as spending money. Ruthie had her hair up off her neck with a ribbon and looked like the woman Clint first met. Sometimes she had eyes that made you believe the water under the bridge might just circle back around again.

The phone still chimed in Clint's ear, whatever it meant. The guy with his pants undone moved toward the bar. Clint wished someone would tell him to zip up. He looked like a fool.

～

"So I talked to my man in Houston," Rex said. "I keep in close touch down there ever since I worked on the offshore rigs to get my stake."

"And?" Clint had heard plenty of Texas talk before.

"He knows an outfit coming through here to hire. They need men to work in the Gulf. Doha City in a place called Qatar, to be exact." Rex smiled as Tim's brow furrowed and his eyes went blank. "Don't worry, Timmer, the names don't matter. What matters is the writing's on the wall, boys. We're gonna go back to Iraq and get that sucker *and* his frigging mustache this time. Long and short, my contact says they're due to need oil men, carpenters, drivers, you name it. You get room, board, and expenses. Plus a fat nest egg when you finish up."

"Like how much?" Clint asked.

"I hear you can come home with eighty grand held back, easy. For one short year. Or two." Rex stood and motioned toward the john. He stepped off and stopped. He stepped back.

"You remember when everybody and his man headed overseas after the first one about what—ten-twelve years back?" Rex pointed up at one of the TV's on the wall. Fox News was showing George W. standing behind a podium, turning a page in a notebook as he spoke. The sound was off, but white captioned text printed off his words below him. "Back when that one's old man was top dog," he said. He squinted back at Clint. "When Buddy Liston came back to Marytown with money enough to buy his own franchise."

"What of it?" Clint pictured Liston in the office, his civic plaque, the open payroll book.

"This's all like that, only better. Know what they're calling Iraq down in Houston?"

"You tell us," Tim said.

"Little Texas." Rex started to laugh but then clamped down when Clint and Tim didn't.

"Liston was flat lucky," Clint said. "That's just the color some guys are." He hoped Moorford know he didn't just mean Buddy. "I heard of lots of guys got took in pretty bad going over there last time. Not to mention, it's life and limb working anywhere in that part of the map since 9-11."

NINE TEN AGAIN

"Fine, you just stay in the car, Mulane," Rex smiled, "the rest of us'll get out and get after it." He hiked at his belt and winked at Tim. "Let me tell you something, she's a new world kicking out there." He pointed at the front door of the Buzz and beyond. "She ain't ever gonna be 9-10 again, boys."

Clint watched Rex disappear in the crowd. Tim was talking, but Clint only heard the last part of what he said.

"—not much in the way of trees, is there? There might not be any wood to build with."

Clint stared out the window where Moorford had pointed. The edges of the glass were frosted and a beer sign blinked in the center, but you could still see through. Pickups came and went on the square and the bar door opened and closed, but nothing changed. And the nothing changed was what Clint saw most clear.

"Maybe we should jump on this," Clint said. "If we both went, we'd have an ear to bend."

"You'd quit Liston?"

"Having Liston on that truck radio is like riding around with your old man for eight hours at a shot."

"What about Ruthie and your boy?"

"What about Phyllis and your girls?"

That shut Tim up—they lived two states away where her folks were. Clint didn't like talking about Ruthie and Chase, not even to friends, but Tim did have a point. When Clint did get hold of Ruthie, maybe they could work something out. Half their problems had always been money, down at the root. Clint looked back at Tim. He was in a different area code on the other side of the table.

"Hey, I didn't mean it mean," he said, shaking Tim's shoulder. "You come back with that kind of money, Phyllis might look at the world through some different glasses then."

"She's found them a new father," Tim said. "He owns a tire shop."

"She remarried?"

"Might as well be."
Neither of them said anything else until Rex came back to the table with another round. That seemed to cheer Tim up, and the three of them shot the bar breeze and counted dream dollars until after eleven, almost like they were all just three plain working men. Rex stepped outside with his phone and came back with the details for a meeting for Tim and Clint: noon the next day at the Country Kitchen in St. Joseph. He seemed damned decent after all the cold-eyed crap Clint had dished his way these past years. Clint wondered if Rex wasn't finally feeling his rightful dose of guilt about living at Clint's daddy's place.

"Well, those eighty miles into St. Joe won't get shorter sitting here," Clint said, standing.

"You driving over tonight?" Tim asked.

"Think I'll drop in on Ruthie. I like a night road anyway."

"For the road then," Tim said, standing up, too. "To the gulf." He raised his bottle.

"To the future," Rex said, reaching for his.

They clinked their bottles and drank. Clint swallowed hard. For one sweet minute there was nothing in his head but a green green future, bank-account time.

Tim wanted to keep toasting and toasting, like in the movies when something big was just about to happen to the heroes. The boat's about to sail. The fight's about to start.

"I love it," he said, "I love it." He held his bottle out. "Here's to Little Texas."

∼

Clint was finishing the last of the road coffee Missy had brewed for him when he saw the first lights of St. Joseph. He wanted to plot out how to play it with Ruthie, but he also knew it wouldn't play to think more than a move or two ahead on her. Nobody could do it. He'd just tell her about

NINE TEN AGAIN

the work deal and the year overseas calm as could be. If the going got wild, he'd show out the unvarnished truth for a change. If you simpled it down all the way, it couldn't be that hard to say. He loved her and he loved Chase.

At the highway 14 intersection he saw the sign: *Welcome to St. Joseph   Pop. 73,990*

Just reading the numbers gave Clint that pinned-down, caged-up feeling. Then a whole string of stoplights by the Whitmore mall popped first yellow and then red ahead of him, and he wanted to whip a fast U-turn and go home. Too many too bright lights, and the trimmed trees stood in rows like pets, and you couldn't smell soil anywhere if your life depended on it. What could Ruthie be thinking of, paying a stranger to live on a high-traffic avenue with a yard narrow enough to pee across and two scrawny Chinese elms for the only summer shade? And all this when Clint still had his five acres with a tangle of woods along the branch creek and good dirt that grew corn six foot tall in ninety days.

He slowed down and squinted for cops. He hated how they waited on the sidestreets with their lights out and radar on, sneaky as raccoons prowling out of the creek bottom on a summer night when the garden grew so quick you almost hear it.

⁓

The next morning the waitress picked up Clint's empty breakfast plate just as Tim walked through the double doors of the Country Kitchen.

"Morning," Tim said. "You don't look well-slept."

"Gotta do it to look it," Clint said, sipping at his coffee. He brushed his hand through his hair. "I'll comb up before our boys show up."

"D'you find somewhere else to drink last night, man?"

"I was over to Ruthie's."

Tim sat down and brushed ashes off the table. "Me, I

woke before the alarm. I think the keys are turning in our locks today, Clint, I really do. Ruthie and the boy okay?"

"Chase was asleep. But she and me came to where the waters up and part, man."

"She didn't buy the idea of you going overseas?"

"I'm a fool. If I quit Liston now after getting my own route, I'll be lucky to work at Shop-Kwik." Clint raised his eyebrows. "Her words."

"Maybe she just wants you close because she'll miss you," Tim said.

"Maybe she just wants to buy that over-priced town shack she rents," Clint said.

Tim opened two packets of powdered creamer and stirred them in his coffee.

"Clint, what if there's nobody like us over there? It's a different deal in those places. Strange churches. I heard they don't even drink. Women can't drive or talk. What'll we have to say to anybody?"

Clint threw a mock punch at his shoulder. "Timmy, Timmy. You think it's still the same world you and me grew up to?"

Tim squinted at the kitchen bar where the tickets hung in rows. He didn't answer.

"It's not a trick question, man. The ones that get ahead of the game, like Moorford, damn his friendly soul, they're the ones know it's not. You check out this cafe right here. All any of these folks have in common is the weather." He pointed outside where sunlight glinted off snow. "That, and whatever's on the tube." He nodded toward a muted TV bolted to the wall. A ball player in a purple jersey quickly crossed himself and then swished a free throw. Fine print news scrolled steadily across beneath him.

Tim ordered and had finished his breakfast when the restaurant cashier walked toward their booth carrying a folded slip of paper. It was a few minutes after twelve. Clint had his hair wet down and his shirt tucked. Tim was watching every car as it pulled into the lot, peering out through his own reflection in the window.

"Mister Mulane?" The cashier looked from Clint to Tim and back.

"What's left of him," Clint said.

"You have a phone message." She handed him the paper and walked away.

Clint read her careful script, small circles above the I's: *Clint, if they's one born every minute your worth a good hour at least, R.M.* He folded the note once and then again.

"Don't tell me they're not coming," Tim said.

Clint shifted in the booth. "They're not coming." He pocketed the note. "Their plane had problems in Wichita."

Tim sagged. "Piss on a cold fencepost, man. I drove all the way here."

Clint squeezed his cup. "Maybe we can meet them next time."

"I'll call Rex when I get home," Tim said. "I'll see what he knows."

"No," Clint said. He dropped a twenty by their tickets. "I'll call. I'll take care of Rex."

When Clint stopped at the turnoff to his place, he realized he was doing things as if he had a plan. But he didn't. He just had things to do, one, and then another. He had stopped and picked up a *For Sale* sign and a contract from Jed Rideout at Tri-Valley Real Estate, without answering any of Jed's questions. That was one thing. Now he left the pickup running and rummaged for the crowbar he kept under a Stihl saw and a gas can. He pounded the sign into the ground with the back of the crowbar. That was another thing. You could read the sign going by either way on the highway.

Behind the house he brushed snow off a mound of straw

and dirt where he and Chase had worked together, banking in the garden vegetables in October. As he raked back the straw, a blue-black crow swooped to a higher perch in the alder tree by the chicken house. The sun slipped behind clouds and Clint's shadow faded. He tossed dirt on the snow as he dug.

The phone in the house rang and Clint leaned on the spade, staring across last summer's broken cornstalks. Smoke from the Randall's chimney spread east across the sky like faded brushstrokes. The phone finally quit ringing, and Clint knelt and stacked vegetables on the straw: dark red potatoes, light green cabbage, purple-top turnips, bright orange carrots.

Clint loaded up the truck, a few cardboard boxes, three wooden kitchen chairs, two lamps, a boombox and TV, the vegetables in burlap bags. He wrapped a quilt around the TV and then tarped down the pickup and then grabbed a rusty hatchet and went into the henhouse. When he came back out, he held a brown hen, dangling by its legs. On a wide stump he swung her down and cut her head off. He clothes-pinned her feet to a line running between two trees.

The sun had set by the time he'd bled and cleaned all six hens. A fire crackled by the bloody stump, and the snow around it was spattered red and littered with brown and white feathers. Clint washed his hands in a drift and packed a large beer cooler with grainy snow and the chickens. The sugary smell of burning entrails smouldered up from the fire.

A few minutes later, as the roadside *For Sale* sign faded behind him, Clint twisted his rearview mirror down so he could see a slice of his face. Both eyes. His pack of stale smokes lay on the dash. He shook three cigarettes out and talked outloud.

"These are the ways you can do it, man. Get out, get even, or get straight. You pack this whole tired state in like you was ready to just this morning and go somewhere newer.

NINE TEN AGAIN

Montana, or Alaska maybe."

He steadied one cigarette on the dashboard. He looked back in the mirror.

"Or, you could go out to Moorford's. It's sure not like you don't know the way. And then what? Call him out right in front of his family?"

He tapped his brights down and back up as a car passed. He laid the second cigarette out. The truck crested a hill, and for a second the lights lit up the farmland ahead. Fallow fields spread out on both sides of the road, the plowed hills rolling away in the dark like huge muscles.

"Or, you could go camp yourself on Ruthie's porch till she talks to you. Tell her when you sell the place, you'll put the money down on the house there and commute to Liston's till you find good work in St. Joseph. Be a goddamn husband and father and quit pissing your life away on dreams you can't tell anybody what they are if they even asked."

He set the last cigarette on the dash. "One. Two. Three." He stared at the eyes in the mirror as if they belonged to a stranger who could reach out and choose for him. The truck leaned around a curve and the smokes rolled together at the far end of the dash.

~

Clint's truck idled behind a clump of blackberries and sumac on a knoll a quarter mile north of the Moorford place. A farmlight cast stark shadows around Rex's house, yard, and barns. Lilac ran along the gravel road in front and up one side of the drive. White board fences divided the barnyard into pens and corrals. Where the worn down frame house that Clint's granddad built had been, Moorford's low brick-front house sported a redwood deck in back and a three-car garage to the side. Only the same tall shade oak stood in the center of the front yard, its bare branches angling into the night sky. Rex's crewcab sat in the plowed drive.

Clint turned his ignition off when he saw the porch light come on. Rex walked out behind his wife and two kids. As they drove away, the exhaust puffed white each time the transmission shifted. Cattle lowed in the distance like a train whistle under water.

Clint listened to his own truck, ticking and snapping, shutting down like the cold iron box it was. He stared from the house on down behind the back pasture and then to the thick line of trees where Till Creek traced away through the bottoms toward the Bighead River. He closed his eyes and conjured all four seasons, appearing and disappearing. It was like seeing the same picture painted a dozen different colors.

Not really that big of a deal, he thought, nothing a thousand others didn't have. Nice house, new truck, white fences. What made it really different was the shade tree. That old oak tree that Clint had climbed and swung from and rested under and raked up after. That fifty-foot oak tree was what made it. Clint felt a hard pull down inside himself that made him think none of the years between those days and this night were real at all. Thirty-one. Thirteen. Just numbers that scrambled up to nothing.

But the shade tree, that was something. It was what he'd loved most when he lived here. It seemed a better than even bet it was what they loved most, too.

A quarter-moon broke over the southeast horizon as Clint walked up the icy drive, the chainsaw balanced over his shoulder, his right hand steadying the long bar. His hood was drawn tight, and the cuffs of his leather gloves were tucked in his jacket sleeves.

"Anybody home?" He waited. A hint of an echo and then the cattle again.

NINE TEN AGAIN

He stretched his hand out and touched the oak tree. Then he stepped far enough away to see the top of it. What little wind there was blew steady from the west. He pushed the primer twice and braced the saw with his boot and pulled three times until it fired. When he revved it, the noise slid higher like a scream. He backed off and the chain slithered on the bar. Clint picked up the saw with both hands and stared at the black trunk. He felt it full for a second, that the tree was every bit as alive as he was and a whole lot older.

He remembered the shapes of it so clearly. It had the same lean to it and the heaviest branches still tended east, like always. Clint knew for certain he could lay it down in under five minutes. He knew it would drop east and a little south, right through the hedge and across the road and the far fence. Moorford wouldn't even be able to get to his driveway.

And then he knew more. He knew he could cut his foot off faster than he could feel the pain, and lie down and bleed to death in the snow, and still not be any more dead inside.

He hit the kill switch and set the saw down. He heard nothing but the wind then, sluffing across acres of snow and cornstalks and trees, sliding across Livingston County like the breath of a hard-sleeping beast no one could see. He gazed up into the net of black branches and grabbed for a limb and pulled himself up by memory, his boots scrabbling against the cold bark.

In the notch of the first limb he stood upright, seven feet off the ground. He pulled and shinnied higher, going from limb to limb, his breath heavy and white in the air. He climbed higher than the farmlight on the pole by the barn. The yard and house below him looked like a lit set on an outdoor stage, waiting on actors.

Clint scrambled up another few feet, as high as he could climb, until the branches swayed with his weight. He stared away from the low white wink of the moon, into the darker night sky. The longer he looked the more stars he could see. He counted at least three white lights, moving too high and fast to be anything that ever landed anywhere. Satellites and such, running errands with no end, taking pictures for somebody. Before he started to edge back down, he looked away from them, too.

In the northern distance the lightshadow from town glowed at the brim of Brissler's Hill. Closer than that, but still far off, Clint could see the ice on Till Creek, thin and slick, glimmering in the moonlight.

THE
WHITE
BEAST

NINE TEN AGAIN

Water pooled on the pavement, but the Porsche handled easily in the rain. The car was still new enough to Roy that he could sometimes feel a boy's thrill in driving it. He tooled around the three familiar curves on Vista Drive, spiralling up the hill to his neighborhood, one hand on the steering wheel, the other holding the phone to his ear.

The serpentine brick wall around the entry to Woodland Heights glistened a purple red in the rain. The late afternoon sky had gone dark gray, and lightning flashed over downtown St. Louis in the distance. The tall buildings and the arch were toys in the flash of light, the city a distant diorama behind glass. The windshield wipers made no noise.

Roy slowed at the entry gate and smiled at the guard, who sat intent over the evening crossword. The guard smiled back and waved, a pencil in his hand.

A tap on the remote and the garage door rose on cue, pulling itself up like a drawbridge. Roy sat in the dim light for a moment, loosening his tie and shoelaces.

The house was silent, empty. Sarah and the kids wouldn't be back from her parents in New York City until late Saturday. Roy had been a little hesitant for them to fly there, but as Sarah said, it had been over a year and a half since the attacks, and the family couldn't quit flying forever.

Twenty four hours to himself. In the family room he sat down and propped his feet up, sipping wine. He reached for the magazine next to him, folded open to the story on the NBA playoffs. Four action pictures were inset at each corner of the page. Spin, slam, fade, dunk. Roy shook his head. They were amazing, really, these guys: miracle men. He would trade places with any of them in a blink. To be able to move like that.

He looked around. Oak furniture, rock fireplace, redwood deck through the window, and then the common woods stretching down and away from the backyard. Hell, he was fine. He was doing all right for himself. Better than all right. And the family. It was good, all of it, good.

Except for the wind and the rain outside, it was quiet. The wind across the roof and around the windows sounded like huge lungs blowing and breathing at his ear. Roy couldn't name the last time he had sat alone in his house and listened to a storm. The magazine fell in his lap.

∽

Roy sat up. He heard nothing now, not inside or outside. He went to the kitchen and sliced cheese onto crackers. In the family room he clicked the TV to ESPN and muted the pre-game show, four suited commentators in jocular argument. A weather advisory scrolled across the bottom of the screen. A tornado watch and thunderstorm warning for Jefferson County.

Roy looked back outside. It was full dusk now and perfectly still. He grabbed the binoculars on the windowsill and picked up his Peterson's guide. This was the best hour for birds. In the morning he seldom had time. He had started a list last fall when they moved in and already had more than twenty species. He slid the glass door open and stepped out on the deck. The air after rain smelled moist and fecund, wet wood, soil, grass, leaves, everything soaked through but too alive to rot. The sky looked formless, as if anything from a sunset rainbow to driving hail could happen next. Roy stepped to the edge of the deck and scanned the trees with the glasses. He heard what he thought was a bluebird, but he didn't see it.

He stopped moving. A young buck and three does stood between a Scotch pine and silver maple, a little way into the woods along the wide grassy path that led to the bluffs. Roy often saw deer in the yard, found tracks in winter, scat in summer, but they still fascinated him. These four sniffed the air and cocked their heads, their ears twitching. The weather had them completely alert in their own world.

Roy walked slowly, keeping the pines at the side of the yard behind him, feeling his feet bend on the ground with each step. It was the way old Al Morissey, his Scout Leader, had told them that Indians walked when Roy was young enough to believe such things, or desire such things. At the edge of the woods he peered from behind the triple forks of a box elder. The deer were still there, twitching, each of them a single tan muscle with eyes.

They let him come closer than he'd ever been. He thought he could smell them, like large wet dogs, yet different. One of them dropped beads of scat as it stared back up the path. At thirty feet, Roy stopped. Their eyes looked like large black marbles, so dark and featureless they could be slowly rolling in their heads. They were so beautiful he couldn't imagine why anyone would ever kill one. And yet he could see why, too. He stared at the fine legs, counted them. Sixteen. Impossibly thin, like taut leather cables.

A quick rush of wind swayed the trees. Roy looked up at the treetops, all bending at the same angle as if the sky pressed them down from above. As he moved his head, the deer bolted. Roy tensed at the drum of their hoofs.

It was almost dark. Roy headed back. His heart beat in his throat and his eyes felt washed and wide. The moment was too physical not to be an emotion, yet he didn't know quite which one. Privileged, he said to himself. Privileged and humbled. He hurried against the coming rain. Triumphant, too, he thought as he climbed the redwood stairs and grabbed the guidebook where he had left it. But not over anything or anybody. He walked in the open door. It was like he had won something without anybody else losing. He closed the door and hung the binoculars up. For an instant something smelled odd as he walked across the dining room. Like urine maybe, or old hamburger left out of the fridge too long.

On screen they were just introducing the starting lineups. He had time for a quick shower. He looked back through the window as he headed toward the bathroom. Lit by lightning, the tops of the trees whipped back and forth, stirring the sky like a dark liquid. A sheet of water slapped the window, and then he couldn't see anything except rain. At the bathroom door he caught another whiff. He thought of the deer again, how close he had been, how quickly they disappeared. Where would they go on a night like this? He hoped they were all right, and then he smiled at his childishness. They didn't need him to help them weather a storm. They were fine. They didn't need him at all.

～

Roy stepped out of the shower, whistling, his skin reddened from the hot water. He reached for a towel but the racks were empty. He bent over into the shower and shook his head dry like a dog. He stepped out into the hall toward the linen closet.

He stopped in mid-step, his mouth open wide, then shut, then clamped shut. The damp hair on the back of his neck moved. An animal stood in the hallway door to the family room. It looked stupid and confused, its long white snout nosing into the carpet, its eyes dark dull beads. It was larger than a cat, but for a moment Roy couldn't think what it was.

NINE TEN AGAIN

The animal moved back and forth in the doorway, as if trying to decide whether to come into the hall. Then it did, and Roy saw the long tail, almost as long as its body, light, scaly, hairless. An opossum. My God, an opossum in his house. He wanted to laugh but couldn't. The creature looked primitive and dangerous, and its smell was as thick as grass clippings in a plastic bag on a hot day. He backed up two steps toward the bathroom. Opossum. He didn't believe they were dangerous, but it smelled almost like a skunk, not as sharp, or as foul, but something like that. Did they carry rabies? What was it doing in here? He remembered the odor when he came in from the deer. The open deck door.

The animal hissed. Roy stood naked in the hallway, dripping on the carpet. Its fur was long and coarse, the tail moving back and forth behind it like a snake. It was impossible to tell where it was looking. Its eyes were as blank as black stones.

Roy stomped his foot on the floor. The animal reared onto its hind paws, still hissing, and opened its jaws. They kept opening wider and wider, so wide that Roy couldn't see the creature's eyes or ears. All he could see were its teeth, two long double rows of them. He had never seen so many teeth. Roy jumped back into the bathroom and slammed the door.

His hands trembled. He picked up a shag throw rug and dried himself as best he could. In a drawer he found a pair of scissors. He grabbed them and a can of hair set from Sarah's side of the cabinet. He looked in the mirror, feeling ridiculous, and yet the animal was lost, in strange surroundings, you couldn't predict something like that. He was sure it was an opossum. He'd seen them on the highways, never sure what they were really, just an odd word that everyone used, a quick low white glimpse and then gone. Marsupials, my God, yes, they were marsupials, like the kangaroos and koalas. And the long bare tail, searching and active like a monkey's.

Jesus, Roy thought, something from another world had washed right up in his hallway. It was fascinating, though, fascinating. But all those teeth. And rabies, if they were in the skunk family, but no, marsupial, even if it smelled like skunk. Maybe that's why it had come in. Maybe it was rabid. He should be cautious. Weren't they supposed to play dead? This one didn't look dead, but alive and fearsome, small, yes, but still, right here inside the house. Roy looked down at his bare toes. He saw Sarah's worn houseslippers under the sink. He stretched them on, working them partway over his feet. He opened the door and peered out with the scissors in one hand and the spray can in the other.

The animal was gone. Roy walked down the hall, spraying the hairset in front of him to counter the strong smell. The storm blew louder outdoors, and Roy heard the pinging of sleet or hail on the windows.

The opossum huddled in the center of the family room, facing the TV, its back to Roy. It looked smaller now, motionless except for the tail. One of its back paws was splayed out behind it and had the shape of a hand. Four clawed toes, but then a black thumb-like digit, shorter and jointed without a claw or nail. Roy cleared his throat. The animal's ears twitched and the snout turned slowly toward him. Roy grabbed the doorknob and pulled the door shut until it clicked.

After he found a towel and dried himself, he dressed and put on his golf shoes and called Animal Control. The dispatcher said it was unlikely anyone could be out before morning, but she assured Roy she would radio his call to the night truck. They would be out as soon as they could, she said. She asked if the animal was rabid. Roy said he didn't know.

He pulled the drapes on the large windows and stared out into the storm. Thunder resounded every few minutes, rumbling in distinct waves, as if the earth somewhere beyond the horizon was breaking apart in stages. Lightning lit up the woods behind the house, the trees still waving, the rain slanting hard from the south.

Roy tried to watch the game on the living room TV but couldn't stay interested. He fixed a turkey sandwich. He thought about the opossum and wondered if he should feed it. He hoped it wasn't pissing or crapping on the carpet.

At halftime, he peeked in through the family room door. The opossum hadn't moved. He set down a plate with the last bite of turkey sandwich and pushed it into the room with the tip of his golf shoe and closed the door again.

Obviously, he had overreacted. It didn't look rabid. Only frightened, probably hungry. Yet he couldn't shake the image of its open jaw and the row upon row of teeth.

He found a dictionary Sarah used for her Cryptograms. He thumbed toward *O*. There was good information on the Internet, no doubt, but the computer was in there, too.

Opossum. That's what he had here. A line sketch depicted the animal in a tree, its tail wrapped around a limb, its young on its back. Roy smiled. He skimmed the text. *Opossum. AmInd. (Algonquian) name, lit. white beast. Marsupial, family Didelphidae. Tree-dwelling. Omnivorous. Ratlike prehensile tail. Female carries its young in pouch. Active at night, pretends death when trapped.*

Roy stared back at the sketch. It certainly didn't look fearful. Perhaps this one in his house was female. It might even have young in its pouch now. Maybe that's why it was angry. That would be only natural.

Roy set the book down and tiptoed through the hall and opened the door again. The opossum hadn't come to the plate. It huddled on the built-in work table along the wall. Roy nudged the plate farther into the room. The opossum came to the edge of the table, facing Roy. He wondered how far it might be able to leap. Not this far, he thought, one eye on the doorway. He squatted down and stared at it, almost at eye level. The opossum moved off again and wiggled in between the computer and the wall. Roy tried to get a glimpse of its belly. The tip of the animal's tail fluttered over the keyboard as its snout sniffed the air. It hissed again.

Roy spoke low, "Easy, easy." The opossum moved to a pile of papers and began to scratch at them, rumpling them towards its belly and then shredding them in quick motions. Roy moved to the chair and grabbed his magazine and rolled it up tightly. A thin line of urine ran along the table and dripped off the edge.

Roy strode across the room, waving the magazine like a club. "Stop it. No. Stop it." The opossum dropped quickly from the table to the chair beside it and then to the floor, six feet away, between Roy and the door now. Roy slapped the magazine against the table. At the loud crack the opossum turned around suddenly and opened its jaws wider than a right angle, displaying its teeth again. It hissed even louder than before.

Roy felt more confident this time. He had the magazine club, he was dressed, his feet were in solid shoes. He could probably kill the animal with one swift accurate kick, but he didn't want to kill it. He just wanted the damn thing out of his house. He backed off two steps, trying to let it calm, hoping he could maneuver around to the door before it did.

As he stared at the animal, the windows all lit with lightning and thunder cracked right behind it. Close, Roy thought, too close. The opossum's body shook as the thunder resounded, as if it were having a fit, its hair bristling in waves, the tail rushing from side to side, the jaws frozen open. Another flash outside, and even before Roy heard the thunder this time, all the house lights went out. The hum of the refrigerator stopped.

Roy tried to count seconds, but his heartbeat was all he

heard and that was way too fast. He backed to the corner, crouching with the magazine in front of him, listening, willing his eyes to see through the dark.

He heard nothing. No hiss. No more thunder.

But it was out there, only a few feet from him in the dark, angry and frightened. No, that was BS. Roy couldn't know anything of what the animal felt. Those things were in him, the anger and fear were his. It, this animal, this opossum, was only teeth. Teeth and eyes and claws out there in the absolute dark on the carpet, with the smell so thick that Roy imagined it was the one thing he could see, a darkness inside the darkness.

Roy could feel his blood, so close to the surface, his soft neck and wrists exposed. He hunched his shoulders and bent forward, wanting armor, a weapon, light, anything but the dark and the smell and the silent teeth he couldn't see. His own breathing was loud. They were sharing the same air, he and this creature, breathing in and out. But where was it? Had it moved?

Active at night. Jesus, it was nocturnal and could see him perfectly well in the dark. This blackness was its element, and Roy was defenseless. He could run for the door, but what if he stepped on it? What if he tripped? He imagined the teeth closing on his hand, his throat, his cheek. Omnivorous. It wouldn't kill him to eat him, but if he stumbled, if he was disabled somehow, here in his house, it might. Roy felt lost, barely sure which way was up or down, lost in a black wilderness right inside his own house.

Sweat coated his body. His teeth chattered. This imagining was worse than anything. It had to stop. He was ten times the creature's size, twenty times. If he stayed in one place, it wouldn't attack. He would wait for his eyes to adjust, wait for the lights to come on. The animal had been heading for the door. It was probably lumbering somewhere else in the house right now, trying to find a way outside. Roy thought his eyes could make out the table across the room now. He stood up straight, trying to pick out the doorway, ready to run to it. He wanted to pray, and that was ridiculous, he knew, ridiculous to pray to be delivered from an opossum. But it was the dark. Anybody would be more afraid in this dark.

He closed his eyes, ready to pray and run and not sure which to do first, and the lights flashed back on. Immediately, the house became a house again. The opossum lay on its side on the floor, drool oozing from its closed jaws. Its legs were stretched rigid, the tail still, a dark watery stain on the carpet behind it.

Roy took one step. The opossum didn't flicker. He walked around it, his hand at his nose. When he was between it and the door, he stretched his shoe out and nudged it, once and then again and once more. It was rigid.

After he drank another quick glass of wine, Roy went to the garage and found a cardboard box and a stiff-bristle push broom. In the kitchen he put on two padded oven mitts. He knelt and shoved the creature into the box with the broom and carried it out onto the deck. In the box it seemed small and harmless, so convincingly dead that he wasn't sure it wasn't. Maybe it had been rabid, or sick, on its last legs, just come into his house to die.

The rain on the trailing edge of the storm was light. Roy rolled the opossum onto the grass and left the box and broom and mitts next to it. On his way back in he flicked on the deck lights. He slid the door shut and gazed back at the animal, its white face shining in the light, motionless on the lawn. If it hadn't moved by morning, he would know. He would take it into the woods somewhere and bury it.

Inside, he busied himself with the mess, spraying a can of carpet cleaner on all the spots and air freshener in each room. He cancelled his request at Animal Control. "The animal is gone," he told the dispatcher. "It's outside now."

After the carpet cleaner dried, he vacuumed. He always hated the loud noise of the vacuum on the rare occasions when the cleaning service used it and he was home, but tonight he didn't want to turn it off. The opossum had seemed so sensitive to noise. He pictured himself chasing the creature down the hallway with the vacuum cleaner. Sears vs. Nature. No contest.

He poured more wine and watched the last quarter of the game. The Timberwolves won. He clicked the set off and walked to the door and stared outside again. The opossum was gone. It had only been feigning, after all. Roy wouldn't have to worry with it in the morning. He left the outside lights on and locked the doors and pulled the drapes closed.

He sat down in the silent house, smelling the pine scent air freshener everywhere. Sarah would notice it the second she walked in. This would certainly be a story to tell her, he thought, but it would change as he told it. The fear he had felt wouldn't fit in the telling. It would just be words, a sketch, like the line drawing in the dictionary.

He didn't want to watch anything more. There was really nothing else to do except go to bed, but Roy didn't want to face that. He stretched out in the chair, staring at his hands, thinking of the opossum's strange back paws, that odd nail-less thumb, so like his own. The fear was over, even the memory of it fading fast now, already thin like a shadow. But in its place another feeling welled up, filling Roy as he sat with his eyes closed in the living room. Lonely. That was the word for it, he thought. Plain ordinary lonely, what everybody just found themselves feeling from time to time. As he said the word in his head, he began to sense sleep moving in from far off. Everything would be fine, soon, in sleep, and then tomorrow, a Saturday, and the family coming back. All the blessings were there to count, if he cared to, and perhaps he should, for there hadn't been any tornado, at least not here. No tornado, or earthquake, or flood, not here, and even the fearsome weather of the war far away, only glimpses of it between the games and shows. Another day done without any real disaster, just an animal, a strange animal, a small one though, here in the house where it didn't belong, but no harm done, really, no houses blown apart the way it sometimes happened, to real people just like Roy, that and worse, which it would do no good to think of, those worse things, not with the family far away, and then on the planes tomorrow. But not today, nothing bad, really, at all, just a day about to end the way it should, and had to, with sleep approaching, and the animal outside, gone for good, although Roy almost missed it now, but still, tomorrow a Saturday, and the family coming back, it was all right, this feeling, just for a few minutes, as the forest of sleep came near. It was all all right, even with this lonely feeling inside, small and wild, loose and afraid.

A COUNTRY VOICE

NINE TEN AGAIN

It's pretty in the garage. Plenty of work space, the radial arm saw and wood lathe against the south wall, lumber racks along the north wall, and in the corner, a wet-dry shop vac. A full-length two-by-six pine workbench across the back wall, with wood vise on the right. Pegboard above and below, with every tool I need. And a shop grinder on the left, to keep everything razor sharp.

Out there, it's not pretty. What's pretty gets torn down. Fast. What's real gets stepped on—sawed off and rooted out. What's true gets turned into TV, one night at a time. Desert Storm or Desert Soap. From the lazyboy, one's the same as all.

But I know the Charlie's still here, lurking at the heart. Those malls full of feel-gooders and their shiny yellow ribbons don't fool me. I know what's pretty and what never could be. This chair could be pretty when it's finished. Mortise and tenon, the joint to last a lifetime. Chisel-pretty. Mine's a beautiful set: quarter-inch to three-inch and every size between, by the eighth. You can split hairs with them. Today I carve another tenon on one end of the back crossbrace. If it's not perfect, I'll start another. Ash is hard, but workable. It takes time to make it pretty. I have time.

⁓

"Chad, do you want lunch?"

That's my wife, Celia. She lives here, too. In the house, not the garage. The garage is all mine.

"Not now, thanks, I'll fix myself something later, honey." I use my city voice, but it's not the one I count on. Every now and then it disappears, and I don't know where it's gone. When it happens, I don't care. It's the others who care.

~

It takes time to dig. Time to sharpen stakes and time to camouflage the pit. Time to crap and time to baste the points with crap.

Takes time to die. Ask Orwell, my best friend, twenty years old, black and beautiful, the way they used to say, with a picture-pretty girlfriend waiting in Athens, Georgia. Maybe she's still waiting.

All my friends knew time. Especially the ones that died. Some turned to spray, a giant red sneeze in the jungle, then silence. Orwell went slow, an ashen grimace turned to gray stone, hanging over my shoulders for a three-hour trek through knee-deep rice.

I save my nightmares for the daytime. Sunlight can really bring the colors out—high resolution terror trips. I study them, learn from them. One sliver of ash at a time. You curl it back against the blade like a single layer of skin, and you watch the grain for clues. Let the blade talk to the wood, find out how it needs to come apart, what kind of chair it wants to be.

Furniture making. It wasn't my idea.

The first VA head-bender, Hodkins, suggested it almost ten years ago, after the first episode—what he called my Breakdown with a capital B. That was a dozen years after I came back. Up until then, I seemed picture perfect—no memory equals no problem. But when my lights went out in '81, Hodkins was who they assigned to me, and he's the one who talked me into furniture. When I finish this chair I'm working on, I'm taking it into the third one, Reilly. I'll carry it into his office, set it down a foot from his desk, and plant myself. I have a stare that makes people remember appointments, calls they need to make.

I know why they're uneasy. They can only guess. The only way to beat Charlie is to psych him out, wait him out. Stare him down.

It's what I can see that creeps them. I look in eyes, I see eyeballs. Out of the head and into the palm, pretty rubber eggs without a shell. I look at hairlines, I can see scalps, shrunk and puckered like hogskin, braids and hanks for the rifle barrel. Show me ears, I can see a string of leather buttons, trader beads back at base camp. Go ahead, invite me over for a backyard barbeque—take a chance on the weird old Vet down the block—let me tend the steaks. When the fat hits the fire, what I see is napalm, the special way napalm burns skin, little blue jelly flames that wrinkle flesh up in layers like twisted black stars.

That's why the neighbors don't invite. They see it in my eyes. Even though they can't say exactly what they see, and I never do. When I talk, if you listen close, you'll hear three things, over and over, in my own code. Name, rank, number. But inside, there's a real person here. Captain Last Laugh. I've got a country voice that only I can hear.

Charlie's in their hearts and in their heads. That's what losing a war means. The enemy crawls inside your skin, fills your veins a pulse at a time. I look around this town, I see the embalmer hard at work. The midnight make-up man in his charcoal suit, working overtime in the small hours. His long fingers at each corner of the mouth, stretching a smile across a scream, patting on a cheap powder base to conceal the nasty wound. The way the survivors like it. All flowers and veils and shiny cars that whisk you right back home to the tube.

Formaldehyde. I smell it everywhere. It's one reason I like to keep the garage door down, even on the nicest days.

"Chad, you want a cup of coffee? You sure you don't want a sandwich?"

Celia again. Sweet indulgent Celia. She still thinks food and drink are what keeps a man going. Food and drink only keep a man alive.

"I'm not hungry. If I want a coffee, I'll get one. Thanks."

She likes to hear me talk. Even if it's only to say I don't need her, in so many words. Talk is what keeps her going.

One clean stroke along the ash and I touch up the blade with the fine wheel on the grinder. Nothing to rush for.

The Marine Corps was my college and the country was my graduate school. Simple lessons, learned well, taken to heart. No hurry. Bodies are made of parts and the parts come apart. Never say die.

They sent me to country, where I learned the language you don't go back on, urgent as Braille. It gave me my voice. The blood brothers spoke it, too. They're all ghosts now, far past earshot, and the VA people here can't hear me, they're clones from the central office. They've been body-snatched and mind-washed, with buttons for balls. I can tell by the way they sit. Charlie at the desk, answering the phone, filling out the forms. That's why I get the treatment I get. They like to start wars, but not to finish them. I'm a finisher, a lifer on duty at the homefront, and it makes their skin crawl. They call me a syndrome and mail me monthly checks.

Behind my back, they watch up and down the block, trying to catch me making too much on my side jobs. I keep the neighborhood pretty, lawns mowed, edged, sodded, trees trimmed and fed, flower beds weeded and blooming.

I do everything but spray. Doctor's orders—no contact with chemicals. In country I got drenched in Orange, the rain that was meant to fry trees and shrivel gooks, weather from hell. Picture a chemical rash, head to toe. Cross sunburn with blood blisters and you're pretty close.

Now they deal with it one piece at a time, the way they do everything. I'm minus a spleen, have two-thirds of a stomach, and one of my kidneys kicks in and out every few months. They pay for the slice and dice, keep the pieces, and send me home.

Let go, let God. I work on my chairs.

"It's Saturday," Celia says, as if I wouldn't know. "You haven't forgotten you agreed to take Marcia to the pool, have you? She's counting on it." She stays in her kitchen, her hand on the inside door to my garage.

"Tell her fifteen minutes."

"Marty wants a ride, too. He's meeting some friends who went to the parade."

Marty's my boy. Fifteen going on thirty-five. He wants to be an accountant, and he will be. He's plotting the points on his success curve already. Topnotch grades and already in the junior jaycees. You'll never catch him in the Marine Corps. He'll tell you right out. He'll tell me. He's not afraid of me. Celia still can get a little afraid of me when I go silent—although I would never hurt her—but not Marty, no sir. He's written the old man off. A carpenter. A landscaper.

Marcia's his sister. Thirteen. A sweet girl. She looks like her mother. I don't know how I came by them all, but I'm in the right place, because they call me father, she calls me husband.

Up and down the block, it's ribbon time. It's flag day in February, everyday, but I smell the lie like bad garbage waiting for Tuesday. Twenty years later they're so sorry, but none of them went to country. And none of them is in Kuwait now. It's mostly the downtown boys, the blacks and the browns, and the G.E.D. crew, just like always. The neighbors have Charlie in their souls, and he's making them hate themselves, the way you win a war in the end. Their smug crap makes me sicker than the Orange. They talk about the wildhairs spitting on us, well, it never happened to me. What happened to me is enough VA paperwork to fill a closet, ten years of cold shoulders up and down the block, and no real jobs after the first two just because every now and then I go silent for a month or so.

If anybody had spit on me, I'd have shoved the back of his nose up his brain on the spot. One sharp move, an open palm, and a straight arm. It takes about two seconds if you know what you're doing. I live in this neighborhood. I know. I tend their lawns. I see their front yards, where the money goes. Their back yards, where the bullshit hides. They never want me at their parties because I bring my eyes. They never ask me about my furniture because they don't understand a simple idea, commitment. It's a four-letter word now. They had to shrink it to fit the screen.

No ribbons on my house. I carry mine in my head. It's for Orwell and the other brothers, and I don't show it to suburban office jockeys who think a big decision is whether to drive the Toyota or the VW downtown for a parade as phony as their lives. The real battle's right here in the neighborhood, but they don't see it. They don't have the eyes.

At night I walk their block, staring into open windows, watching the screens flicker the same way their eyes do if you look at them too hard. Any man in my squad could have taken them out, a family at a time, without so much as a scream.

I switch to the three-eighths, squaring the corners of the tenon cleaner than machine-work. I let the grinder run all the time. I love the fine light whirr it makes, like the first breeze in the elephant grass, the one you only hear right before the enemy's all over you.

That's the kind of thing that makes you really listen.

─⌒

Marcia swims backstroke for the junior high team. She hits the school pool all week and then the University fieldhouse on the weekends. I usually wait an hour for her in the car. Today it's snowing like there's no tomorrow. I smoke and watch people, figuring the disguises. A charter bus pulls up and loads a basketball team from somewhere, baby-faced kids, all legs and hands.

Marty took off with two of his hotshot friends, headed for the mall or wherever. He's ashamed of me, doesn't like his friends to see me—he'd have to explain. He'll never have a disability. None of them will. They're on their way. They're middle-distance hurdle runners, and they're good at it. Adjustment city. Where we all live now.

With Marcia, it's too soon to tell. She loves me. She listens to my city voice and settles for that, like her mother. Celia's given up on the big probe. She's called it a draw. I'm here and I'm not. It could be worse.

I lock the car and stroll over to the fieldhouse, stretching my legs and breathing cold snowy air. I step inside and sit on a wooden bench in the hallway outside the pool. I like the moist smell of chlorine in the air. At the end of the hall, a co-ed walks away from the towel counter on her way to the lockers. She's soaking wet in her high-riding bathing suit and has a big towel wrapped up around her head, but from back here, I'm telling myself it all looks pretty damn good. My luck, too, she bends over to brush at something on her foot, and I'm hearing that old bar song: Bend down low, I'll show you what I know. She straightens up fine. As she turns to go into the locker room, she pulls the towel loose and shakes her head.

It's Marcia. It's not her bathing suit, but damn if it's not her. I look away and hit the door fast before she sees me.

I'm back in the car and done with two more cigarettes by the time she comes out. We start home like it's any other Saturday. I keep staring at her, wondering how the hell I could have made a mistake like that.

I reach out and pat her on the shoulder. She's got a thin neck, smaller than my hand.

"What's the matter, Dad?"

"Nothing, I'm just thinking about how quick you're growing on me."

She smiles. "I'm thirteen. I'll be fourteen next summer."

"I don't mean the numbers," I say. But I can't say what I do mean, either. While I'm puzzling that, I tune into the tag end of a mind movie I never wanted to see again. Charlie's little whores, Orwell called them. More than once he and me passed a couple back and forth all night long like candy. This one girl I'm thinking of, though, we buried at morning light. I start to see her face in my head, and she's alive, but I know where it's leading. I crank it all back down and practice my control. The city voice will get me through this. That's what it's for.

"How'd the workout go?" I ask her.

"Fair," she says. "Just fair." She runs her fingers through her hair. It's mostly dry now. "It's weird. Even the slightest change can throw me off. I had to borrow a suit from Vicki Sellen. I left mine at home. I just slogged through it today."

"Good for you," I say. "Win or lose, my girl suits up for the game." It sounds lamer than yesterday's gum, but she smiles anyway.

She saves me and turns on the radio. She stares out the window the rest of the way home, moving her head to the beat of whatever song comes along. I'm talked out, and it takes everything extra I have to keep that morning memory covered down. I distract myself with watching the Charlies in the other cars. Traffic's heavier and slower than

NINE TEN AGAIN

it should be, the last of the parade crowd struggling home on slick roads.

~

At home I remember my chair. I try to concentrate on what I want it to look like. If I finish cutting the tenon, I'll turn one of the legs on the lathe tonight.

Marty comes home at dinner time and strolls through the garage like he's the one who pays the mortgage. He says hello with one of those smirky smiles that looks like he learned it from a clothes ad. I stare at him. All his clothes have brand names and designer names printed on them. Every step he takes is an ad for something.

The tenon isn't perfect, so I can it. I pick another piece and measure and mark it. I saw it to length and sand the ends. But something's not right — my palms are sweaty. It's a sign I remember, and it makes me cautious. I work with my back to the wall.

When the sun gets low, I go out to check the vehicles for the night. As I lock Celia's Buick, I notice the yellow ribbon. Bright and brassy, and waving from our mailbox at the curb, just like all the others. Somebody thinks they're funny but they're not.

It could be Leese, two houses down. I stopped doing his lawn last year because he needled me about how able-bodied the local disabled vet seemed. I quit him without a word. I don't have to take that crap. Leese would be the one to hassle me about the ribbon thing. After I quit doing his lawn, he put gravel in his front yard like we were in goddamn Phoenix or something. He told people that's why he didn't need me anymore.

I untie the ribbon slowly, watching up and down the block, from one house to another. All the long-distance patriots, one eye on the war news and the other on the prime rate. I know where they live. I was one of their investments that went sour.

I want them to know me, so I stand at the curb, enjoying the winter sun, and I eat the frigging thing. You can do anything if you want to. It's all will. I bite off small sections and lather them up with spit and swallow them whole. It takes some time, but I'm not going anywhere.

⁓

"What took you so long, honey?" Celia asks. Dinner is half over. But they've learned not to wait on me. Daddy's moody.

"What took me so long is I ate the stupid ribbon Leese must have put on our mailbox," I say. I sit down and serve myself spaghetti.

"You what? Which ribbon?"

"Somebody tied one of their toy ribbons on our box. I put on a little show for them. I ate it. Have you got any parmesan?"

Celia goes for the cheese. Nobody says anything.

Marty makes a mistake, though. He starts to laugh. If people laugh at you, it's a sign of disrespect. It's a sign that what's important to you is a joke to them. Most days in town you can hang your head out the car window, and that's what you'll hear. It's not the traffic rumbling, it's the sound of thousands of people, laughing at each other from dawn to dusk. In country, we chose what we laughed at with care.

I look at my palms. They're covered with sweat, little beads popping out all across the life line. Or the love line. I get them confused.

"What's funny?" I ask him. "It's funny I know the difference between a real war and a mini-series? That's funny to you?"

I give him my eyes, but he's the only one they never bother. I think it's a basic lack of imagination on his part. When I see this, I feel like a failure as a father, like I should throw this one back in the scrap pile and try again. When people lose their imagination, they're finished. They're doomed to live in only one world.

"No, it's not that," he says, reaching for the garlic bread. Celia hands me the parmesan.

"Well?" I shake the cheese over my plate.

He makes another mistake. He tells me the truth.

"I'm laughing because I know who put the ribbon out there."

I set the parmesan down, but I keep my hand on it. "I'm listening."

"I did. I took it off of Rob's car when he brought me home. I thought it looked good there. They handed them out at the parade today. It's not a big deal. I don't know what your problem is, Dad."

I squeeze the cardboard shaker harder than I mean to. It collapses and parmesan powders out across the table. Marty laughs at this, too. Everything strikes him funny today.

"Maybe you'll find out what the problem is," I say. I fold my napkin and stand. I look at Celia and Marcia, but it's like trying to pick the villagers from the gooks. You get tired trying.

In the garage I try to work, but it's no use. I sit and watch the sweat on my palms spread up my arms. I feel like the wolf-man in the old movies, watching hair grow, waiting for fangs and claws. My years of city fat are melting away like butter in a skillet.

I talk to myself out loud, using my city voice, but it won't stand the test. It sounds like the fake it is. My country voice talks to me in my head like a brother would, watching out for me. You're missing the clues, it says. What's wrong in this picture, it says. I look for colors too bright, things out of place that give away even the most careful setup. I know I'm slower than I was, and sicker, but I still have moves. The imagination. The eyes. Some things don't go.

I take down the three-inch and hone it till it whines. Weapons have a life all their own. Every soldier knows that.

The sun sets in the suburbs. I watch it through the window in the garage door. I sit in the darkness on the old sofa where I sleep on the worst nights. I could be thousands of miles from anywhere. Celia comes to the door once, but I manage to tell her I'm into something I need to work out on my own. That's counselor code for leave me alone. The city voice is on its last legs.

I tie my hair back. I pull it as tight as I can, as if I'm taking in all the slack, as if I could erase every line that twenty years of bullshit have put in my face. I pull on my work gloves.

Hours drift by. I watch sawdust, floating in the light the low moon casts through the window. I turn the chisel in my hand, staring at the dim silver glow that dances on the blade.

The house gets still, all of them in their own little beds, their private dreams. The moon sets early. Every day has a midnight.

―

Every dream has one, too. The boy would have to be the first to go. He's the most dangerous to me and to others. He's sound asleep on his back, and I crush his neck with the side of my hand before he has time to cough. His eyes go milky, and I remember the feeling: no feeling allowed.

I measure my steps. The hallways look familiar, as if I'd been briefed on them in my sleep. The woman is on her stomach, so it's not quite as simple. I lean my knee into her and push her face in the pillow and wait for the slack.

The girl wakes up when the door opens, and she surprises me because she doesn't act afraid. But she's no different, tomorrow she could take my brothers out with a wad of stolen plastic wired between her legs. My hand fits around her throat like I'm shaking hands with a fat man. I send her back to wherever she came from. No blood here either.

I check the other rooms. I search the garage because I remember there's supposed to be someone out there, but it's empty. I drag them out on the concrete floor and stare out the slit in the door at enemy terrain. In the distance, I hear vehicles moving, but there's no telling whose. I don't know how far behind the lines I am.

I retrieve the bedsheets and wrap them. I stash all three of them in the freezer. I stand watch until dawn by the narrow window. When I get sleepy, I unroll my smokes and put tobacco strands under my eyelids. They burn like iron filings.

Dawn comes at 0700. The street is still deserted. Now I can sleep.

A little after nine o'clock, footsteps wake me from dreams as thick as syrup. Someone knocks on the front door to the house. I wipe my eyes and steady my breath. The enemy could be on patrol, looking for his dead.

I creep to the garage window. There's two of them. One tall, fat, male. One short, female. No weapons visible. Only pamphlets in their hands. They knock again, and then turn away slowly. I move into the house on the balls of my feet. I open the front door, just enough for them to notice. They're halfway down the walk, but they turn back.

I retreat behind the couch. I ready my weapon.

"Hello? Mr. Wyman? Mrs. Wyman? Anybody home?"

I hear the treachery beneath the words. I can match it.

"Who is it?" My voice cracks, sounds foreign.

"It's Leona Reed and Fred Bidd." They cast long shadows on the carpet. "We're visiting your neighborhood on behalf of the Assembly of God worldwide ministries.

Do you know about the Old Testament prophecy for the coming days of war and doom? Do you know God provides a forthright explanation for all the suffering we see around us?"

Missionaries. The oldest trick in the world. I swallow slowly, trying to remember the accent. I relax the muscles in the hand that holds the chisel. Timing is everything.

I imagine them sprawled across the floor side by side, head to foot, ready for the sheet. It's like peering two minutes into the future, a gift if you pull it off. I make myself see it. The tall one first. And the short one before she screams.

"Come in," I say. "The door's open."

I wait. Patience is pretty.

I hear someone behind me. It's Marcia, stepping into the hallway, half-asleep, her eyes squinting. She's in her pj's, carrying a box of Celia's tampons, on her way to the bathroom.

"Dad?" She puts the box behind her as if I'd never seen such a thing before. She takes a step into the living room. "Is someone at the door?"

The hinges on the storm door squeak as it opens. They need oil.

A SILVER CLOUD

NINE TEN AGAIN

81345655 space .902 space 041673 Penny pulled her fingers from the keyboard. She had just typed in her own date of birth, and she shook her head, shocked that it belonged to someone else, too, as if it had been stolen from her, even though she had met people born on that same day before. But this was someone she would never meet, someone else who was about to turn thirty this month.

The white plastic keys in front of her gleamed like rows of teeth with little labels. She listened to the other keyboards around her, a chorus of muted clacking, like dozens of baby birds, pecking at the pieces of their own shells.

"Ms. Jeffson?"

Penny turned to see her sector manager, Frederick Boston, standing next to her.

"Can you come to my office for a moment, please?"

Penny had never been inside Boston's office, and as she followed him toward it, she clenched her hand until her palm hurt. She couldn't help remembering the day only six months before, when a plainclothes policewoman led her to the employee lounge to tell her that her nine-year-old, Robbie, had been rushed to Mercy Hospital. He'd been shot in the hip on his way home from school on a warm fall afternoon, a picnic day. Caught in a crossfire, the papers said, gangs shooting at each other, settling scores. The policewoman had bought her a Diet-Slice after telling her the news. Penny couldn't remember if she'd paid her back.

Three of the office walls were glass and stopped just short of the ceiling. Penny sat in the chair Boston motioned her toward, glancing out across the long rows of her co-workers' terminals. Boston settled in behind his desk. It ran almost the full length of the room. Once behind it, he looked like a pilot or some sort of commander.

"Is anything wrong?"

"Of course, that's in essence what needs to be known, Ms. Jeffson. Your work hasn't been meeting quotas. Are you well?"

Penny let her breath go. It wasn't anything about Robbie. "I'm better now," she said. She felt herself smiling too fully and stopped. "I did have problems at home last fall." Penny felt sure Boston must know what had happened to Robbie, although they had never spoken of it.

"In addition to a relatively high error rate and recurrent punctuality problems—" he paused, flipping a pencil between his fingers end for end. "Do you know you've exhausted all of the sick leave you've accrued?"

"I've talked to Marie Restor about my problems with the bus schedule," Penny said. "We discussed those problems. As far as the leave goes, I really was sick."

"Of course. However, as I'm sure you know, sick leave is, in truth, a privilege, not a right. Its prudent use by an employee is to us a key indicator of reliability and productivity."

Boston stared just beyond Penny, and she couldn't quite catch his eye. She turned and looked over her shoulder. Next to his diplomas, a framed photo of him in waders and a fishing hat hung on the wall. Two of his fingers were hooked in the gills of a large gray fish that hung at his side.

"Are you staring at something?" Penny asked, turning back to face him.

"Sorry." Boston smiled and looked down and then directly at her. "To be perfectly frank, it's a technique from a management seminar. One I've obviously not mastered." He smiled again, as if his honesty had put him at ease and should have the same effect on her.

"I'm just not sure I understand what you're saying."

"I'm afraid that for the reasons I've outlined, Home-National Indemnity will no longer require your employment after April 4th. That's two weeks—" He looked at his desk calendar and then his computer screen, nodding to himself. "From this coming Friday." Boston handed her three sheets of paper as he spoke. "This is our standard separation agreement," he said. "Nothing out of the ordinary at all. Please sign and return it to Ms. Restor by week's end."

"You're letting me go?"

"In a word, actually, I'm sorry to have to say that, regrettably, yes, your understanding of the situation is correct."

"Because of the sick leave?"

Penny slid forward in her chair. She saw Boston's eyes flicker down and then away. She remembered what she had heard in the rumor mill. Boston played around.

"No, no. Not only the sick leave. Surely, I made myself clear."

She stood up, smoothing her skirt, the papers in her hand. As she turned to leave the office, she noticed the box of designer tissues on the edge of Boston's desk near her chair.

~

"Only three weeks." Mitch Royal, an underwriter, batted at the newspaper he held and grinned at Penny as he spoke. The headline announced the fall of Baghdad. He slapped the paper down on the lunch table. "It's a great day for the U.S of."

"It really is," said Melissa, a co-worker from Penny's section, 2-L, and Penny's closest friend on the floor. "We did what had to be done and we did it faster than they said we would." She bit into a pressed turkey sandwich she'd heated in the microwave.

"You're awfully quiet today, Penny," Mitch said. "You're not one of those gloom-and-doomers, are you? Looking for the black lining in a silver cloud?"

Penny stared past him through the window at the winter sky. Either the window or the sky looked dirty, tinged.

"Isn't it the other way around?" Melissa asked.

"Mitch is being sarcastic," Penny said.

She felt isolated from both of them. If she told any of her co-workers she'd been fired, they would act sympathetic, and probably feel so, but then they'd find reasons to avoid her. Even Melissa. Penny had seen it happen, even been on the other side of it, although she had never admitted that to herself before.

"You don't look well, girl," Melissa said. "Have you seen yourself?"

"I don't really feel well," Penny said. She paused. "Girl." She was used to how differently Melissa treated her whenever an unattached man was around. "I guess I've never come back completely from whatever that bug was I had at Christmas-time."

Mitch stood and looked down at both of them with a grin that seemed to say he thought he could pursue either on a moment's notice, and probably successfully. Melissa had confided in Penny that she and Mitch had made love once in a locked sixth-floor conference room, but apparently little had developed from that. Penny knew that for many of the men in the office, any of the single mothers at work were exciting enough for that. Penny had never told Melissa she had heard Royal and another underwriter talk and laugh to themselves once when they hadn't known she was anywhere near. Royal had been sarcastic then, too: "Who wants to traipse home with them and learn the gruesome details? The kids, the bills, those photo albums they always stash in the closet." Penny remembered his callous comment nearly every time she saw him smile, which he did again now, at both of them. Only Melissa smiled back.

"Cheer up, Penny," Mitch said. "You could be overseas yourself. They station women damn near at the front lines now. Don't you know that?"

"That's going too far, I think," Melissa said, mostly to Mitch.

"I know about the front lines," Penny said.

Melissa glanced over at the wall clock. "Three till, time to head back," she said to Penny.

Penny stood up slowly. She was thinking again of the day the policewoman came and how unbelievable it had been to her, and still was most days, that her boy had been shot. She stared at the neat knot on Mitch's tie.

⁓

When the log-out message flashed on Penny's screen at the end of the shift, she typed the codes wrong and had to start over. It took a full three minutes extra.

She gave up on hurrying for the first bus and slowly pulled on overboots and her old suede coat, the one she kept wearing even though it was worn now and out of style. It had been a Christmas present to herself ten years ago, the December Robert left, when she was pregnant with Robbie but hadn't told Robert yet. If she had told him, he might have stayed, or not, but she wouldn't tell him after he left. With the money she had set aside for a leather coat for his Christmas, she had bought herself a suede one instead.

It was several blocks from her building to the bus stop, and halfway there Penny realized that she was seeing the sleepers on the sidewalk more clearly than usual. Were there always this many? She had been so excited for her first year working right in the heart of downtown Kansas City, the only real city she had lived in, but somewhere over the course of her years there, it had changed for her. It was as if it had split into two cities, horizontal and vertical. In the tall buildings like the Home-Indemnity Tower, real people worked, the ones with jobs, families, homes. And down on the pavement was the horizontal world, people asleep, drunk, drugged out, or once in awhile, actually dead. Rush hour was the craziest time of all because the two worlds had to cross, and anything might happen then. A beggar might steal your clothes, your credit cards, your smile, and go right back to your job and home, and then you'd be stuck on the street in the horizontal world.

Penny walked around the swollen ankles and canvas shoes of an old woman propped up against a parking meter. She wore a rectangular white cardboard box like a coat, with holes punched out for her arms. Penny avoided the woman's rheumy eyes. She thought of the two worlds again. She could almost feel the fear and envy floating between them, like the thick cobwebs in her mother's attic in the old house in Grand Island.

The separation papers made her purse feel heavy, leaden. She wished she could just hand them to the woman at the parking meter and walk away.

~

Two blocks from her apartment Penny recognized the large man sprawled across the sidewalk. She passed him nearly every evening. He wore large rubber galoshes with missing buckles and held out an open coffee can to every passerby with the one garbled word: "Change?"

The letters stitched in red thread across his blue cap said "Ralph." In her mind Penny called him that, although she had no idea if it was really his name, and she had never responded to him or given him money.

As Penny came near him tonight, her vision floated up to the windows above her, rising like rows of sullen, rectangular eyes. She felt queasy and light-headed. She stopped when

Ralph held the can up. She shocked herself when she spoke to him. "Stand up," she said.

Ralph's bloodshot eyes registered surprise, too. He heard her. And she believed he recognized her, from all the other nights she had passed him. She wondered if he had any name for her in his mind. He slowly lowered the can back down to the sidewalk as if it were heavy, although Penny saw it was empty.

"Please, just stand up. Do you need help? If you just get up, I'll give you some change."

Ralph shifted his weight on the pavement. He braced his hands on the wall behind him. Headlights glinted off windows and car mirrors as if some large whole light had shattered into small rough shards. Penny squinted and looked away from him while he struggled to his feet.

A scrawny teenager with the hood of a purple sweatshirt drawn tight around his face gestured at Penny from the alley across the street. He made a loose fist with one hand, thrusting his middle finger back and forth in it. When Penny glared at him, he raised his eyebrows and unzipped his pants several times as if asking a question. He was obscene, but he looked timid to her, like a deranged purple rabbit ready to run at the slightest scare. Still, Penny gripped the plastic ballpoint pen in her coat pocket. She carried one ever since the self-defense course she had enrolled in after Robbie's accident. She had quit after the first class, but clicking the pen on and off in her pocket now, she remembered part of the lesson.

"Go for the eyes," the instructor had told them. "The eyes or the crotch," she had said, demonstrating both an overhand and underhand thrust.

Ralph pulled himself to his feet with a groan, leaning on the wall. He lurched two steps toward Penny, his galoshes scraping on the sidewalk. The kid in purple walked backwards down the block, still working his zipper up and down like a toy.

Penny let the pen go and reached in her purse. She held out a dollar, staring at Ralph's gnarled hand as it reached toward her. Half of the two smallest fingers were gone, and the tips of what was left looked as pink and shiny as babies' toes.

"Is your name Ralph?" she asked, looking back up at his eyes.

He took the bill and wavered in a small circle. "Bad feet," he said.

Penny looked down at the galoshes and then back at his hat. "Ralph?"

"Swollen," he said. He put the bill in his coat pocket. "Thank you."

From his other pocket, he pulled out a quart bottle of beer with no cap, holding it toward her as if the two of them might have something to celebrate. He shuffled his leg, the galosh dragging awkwardly. A few drops of beer splashed on Penny's coat.

She jerked and patted at the spot. He pulled his bottle away, blinking rapidly, and then staggered backward into the wall and slid slowly down it, sitting again.

Penny pulled another dollar from her purse and put it in the can next to him before she walked away. His voice trailed on behind her, one word at a time.

"Sorry for your coat," he said.

～

The kitchen timer rang after thirty minutes, their agreed-on signal for bedtime. Robbie folded the spelling list he had been practicing at the kitchen table while Penny had pretended to read an anatomy textbook. He usually didn't want her help with his schoolwork, but he liked them both to sit quietly at the kitchen table and study at the same time. Penny normally liked it, too, but tonight the photos in the book looked as foreign as snapshots from the moon. She

NINE TEN AGAIN

tried to concentrate on what to do about her job, but that made no more sense than the photos. Penny had dropped out of nursing school years before, but she had kept her textbooks.

"Can we steam some stamps off?" Robbie asked. He folded the list one more time and closed it in his book.

"Not tonight, hon. I'm too tired. And it's bedtime."

Robbie had begun a stamp collection at Christmas, and Penny saved the mail for him. They steamed the stamps off with a kettle, and he pressed them behind plastic in a photo album.

"We haven't for two weeks." He grabbed the stack of empty envelopes Penny had rubberbanded together on the counter.

"How about you get ready for bed and then you can look through them. We'll take them off tomorrow night. C'mon, I'll put them on your bed."

After he brushed his teeth and pulled on pajamas, Penny stayed in his room and counted for him while he did the exercises the doctors prescribed. He had a long thin stairstep scar up and down the outside of his leg where they had operated to repair his hip, but as she watched him do the exercises more easily and quickly than just a few weeks before, Penny was able to believe that except for the strange scar, he really was going to come through it all right.

"Ten," she said. It was the last repetition of the last exercise, the hamstring stretch. He turned and smiled at her.

"I'm a good kid," he said. It was what he said almost every night at the end of the routine. She didn't know how or why it had occurred to him. His eyes gazed easily on her and his smile was without a trace of guile or bitterness.

"Silvery," she said, half under her breath.

"What?"

"Your eyes," she said. "They look silvery when you're sleepy."

"You're weird, Mom." He undid the envelopes. She sat

on the edge of the bed while he sorted through them. In five minutes he was asleep. She kissed his forehead for a long time, hovering over him with her lips just grazing his skin.

~

Penny clicked the remote through the channels twice before she stopped on a country video station. She stretched out on the couch to open her mail. A third hospital bill. Even after the insurance, she still owed way too much. The rest of the mail was catalogs and credit card offers. She set the stamped envelope aside. She poured a glass of wine.

As soon as the rates changed, she dialed her mother's number in Grand Island. Her mother answered on the first ring, full of news about some guys Penny had gone to high school with who had been arrested on drug charges. A meth house right there in the hometown. She said that the local news showed police in white spacesuits in the front yard. Penny tried to let her mother know what had happened at work, but her mother kept saying how thankful she was that Penny had a job. Penny hinted as strongly as she dared about moving back with Robbie. Lord knows, I'd love to have you two closer, her mother said, but what would you do here?

While she listened, Penny scribbled on the February page of the monthly appointment journal Melissa had given her at the office Christmas party. Her mother agreed that home would be a safer place to raise Robbie, but we're not like we used to be here either, she said. Crazy things happen every day, she said, and then she returned to her story of the meth house and the space suits. They talked twenty minutes, and Penny didn't tell her that she had lost her job.

She set the phone on the floor and wrote on the blank pages of the journal, anything that came to her mind. On the March page, the beginnings of a letter to her mother, in

April, lyrics from the Video Channel, in May, an alphabet song she knew from Sesame Street years before.

A beautiful woman started a song on the video channel: "Honey, you pulled a fine-tooth comb across my heart." The woman wore a tight dress and hand-tooled cowboy boots. "I need to pick up the pieces, find a new place to start." She walked down the center of a railroad track.

～

The alarm wouldn't go off for another hour. Light glared from the lamp on the end table. Penny opened her eyes and looked at the scribbling on the June page of the appointment book wide open on her lap. It looked like something one of those people who have to use their toes or teeth might have written. Then Penny flinched at an even worse thought, a hazy image of Robbie in a wheelchair. He could have been that way. If the bullet had been an inch higher, the orthopedic surgeon said. Penny sat up on the couch, blinking, taking a sudden deep breath.

She hadn't signed the separation papers and she wouldn't. Boston always came to work early. Melissa said he was there once when she came in at six-thirty. Penny could go in and face him, convince him to change his mind. If necessary, she would beg him. She would pay her bills, save a small cushion before she quit, and then go back to nursing school. They would always need nurses, even in Grand Island. She turned the alarm off. Before she dressed, she called the babysitter who walked Robbie to school and asked her to come early.

As Robbie poured out cereal and milk, Penny told him he would have to be by himself until Jeanine arrived in just a few minutes. Then she bent to the table.

"Wish your mom a special good luck wish today, honey," she said.

"Good luck, Mom." Robbie kissed her and she turned

her face so she wouldn't mess her lipstick. He didn't ask why she wanted a special wish or what she might need good luck for.

In the hall she wiped a drop of milk from her cheek.

～○

Except that he wore a different suit and looked clean-shaven, Boston could have been in his office all night. Penny could tell by his expression he'd hoped not to talk to her again so soon.

"Could I speak with you a moment, Mr. Boston?"

"Briefly. Certainly. What brings us in so early today?"

Penny draped her coat over the back of the chair farthest from him and sat down, composing herself. She repeated it all to herself. She just needed to explain about Robbie and show her resolve. Hearing her story firsthand would be far different from reading Marie Restor's quarterly supervisory reports. But Boston spoke first.

"I hope I didn't seem brusque yesterday, Ms. Jeffson. Letting an employee go is without a doubt my least favorite task on any day. But it comes with the territory."

"I can understand," she said. "But you see, I just have to keep my job. Not for myself, but my son. He's just gone back to school, and I depend on the insurance. I know I've been distracted, but I'll do better. And I promise I won't miss any more time."

Boston shifted in his chair, scratched his ear. "Look, Ms. Jeffson—"

"Penny," Penny said, working at a smile.

"Penny. I completely relate to your concern about the insurance. But you'll be eligible to continue your coverage under the COBRA option. For a time. It's all clear in the agreement."

The separation papers jutted out of her open purse on the floor. Penny reached down for them, trying to still the trembling in her hands. As she leaned over, she sensed her skirt ride up. She shifted in the chair, pulling it down as best she could. Boston stared at her.

She held the papers out in front of her knees, gazing at the small print on the first page. She had heard the COBRA plan could cost five hundred a month.

"May I?" He half stood and extended his hand. She gave him the papers. He glanced over her shoulder through the door before he looked back at her.

"Perhaps I could rack my brain and go over this again and see if there's any other possibility here. But in the meantime, I need some copies made. If you would just run them off for me in the 2-L copy room? I'll check on you in a few minutes."

Penny nodded as Boston reached in a drawer and pulled out a manila folder.

"And since it's so early," he glanced at his watch, "you'll need a key." He reached back in the drawer and held out a key, too.

In the copy room, Penny turned on the lights and the copier. The machine message read, *Copier Warming Up / Ready in 5 Minutes*. She opened the manila folder.

The machine message had just changed to 1 *minute* when Boston came to the door.

"Yes, Penny, I believe I have come up with an alternative," he said as he closed the door behind himself, holding the papers up. Penny didn't speak. "I've tentatively changed your termination to probation. It only lacks your signature, and mine, to make it official. We'll be monitoring your attendance, and your performance, weekly for the next three months."

Penny saw him in his waders, standing on the dock with his fish.

"The folder's empty," she said, pointing at it on the machine.

"Did that surprise you?" He raised the company papers in his hand again

"What do you want?" she asked.
"What we all want," he said. "Compliance."

∽

Penny came out of a stall in the women's room and gazed at the flawless white surface of the sink. She turned the water on and let the basin fill, trying to clear her head. If she didn't tell right now, today, this morning, would anyone believe her later? Posters on every floor had numbers to call about it, but Penny didn't know anyone who'd ever dialed them. She pictured the diplomas again on Boston's office wall.

She looked in the mirror. She felt her teeth grind as she grabbed the sides of the sink, looking at the basin, imagining Boston's face in the water. She spread her fingers, jabbing them at his eyes, willing him blind and bloodied. Water sloshed onto the floor. She batted lightly at the sink, but the face was gone in the swirling water.

The restroom door opened and Penny froze. It was Melissa.

"Are you all right, Pen?" she asked. She looked from the water on the floor to Penny in the mirror. Penny looked at her own reflection again. The rage face was gone. All she saw was her hair, flattened on one side, her mascara, smudging below her eyes.

"I think so," she said. She tried to smile. "Yesterday was a bad day."

Melissa set her purse on the counter and opened it with a flourish like some sort of magician's bag. She wet a tissue and wiped at Penny's mascara. She took a brush and pulled Penny's hair back into place. Penny closed her eyes. An old-fashioned word came to her mind. Comfort. Melissa was offering that to her, without even knowing what for.

"How's Robbie doing?" Melissa asked. "He's caught up in school now, didn't you say?"

"Yeah, he's much better. Thanks. He does his leg exercises like a trooper."

Melissa grinned. She turned the drain stop on the sink. "None of it's easy, is it, woman?" Penny shook her head. "But you're here early now, and yesterday is yesterday's business. Today's a new one," she said.

Penny turned back to the mirror. Melissa picked up Penny's coat from the floor, patting at the waterspots on it. Penny hadn't noticed it had fallen.

"I really love this coat," Melissa said. "My sister has one just exactly like it."

Penny grabbed at the coat. "You don't understand anything," she said. They held the coat between them for a moment. "You don't have a clue, Mel."

Melissa let go. "Hey. Excuse me all around the block. Maybe Mitch has it right. You wouldn't see a silver lining if it fell on you. You've had a tough break. But you don't have to turn on your friends."

"Boston put me on three-month probation," Penny said. "I'm being monitored weekly. Just like in the beginning." It was all she could say. The iceberg's tip. She wanted Melissa to guess at everything under the surface.

"I'm sorry," Melissa said. "I didn't know that." Then she winked. "Hell, just flash the lech a little leg every week. It'll keep him happy."

Penny's hand flew up and slapped Melissa's cheek. Melissa backed up two steps, her eyes wide and instantly filmed with water. Then she stepped forward again and slapped Penny right back. Penny staggered, half-sitting on the counter behind her.

"It's not you," Penny said, her hand against her face. "I'm sorry."

Melissa stepped to the door and turned around.

"You and your precious coat can go to hell. You think you're the only one grits your teeth four days to get through five? In case you forgot, I have kids waiting on my paycheck, too, two of them." She was almost screaming. She lowered her voice. "Maybe they haven't been in the newspaper for anything, but Josh takes insulin twice a day and Amber needs braces for three years to fix her overbite."

Penny turned around and clenched her eyes shut. When she opened them, the door in the mirror was closed.

―∽―

Penny logged on her terminal twelve minutes early, trying to read the supervisory memos she seldom had time for. She dangled her arms at her side, letting her hands relax. She pulled a new pile of entry forms on the corner of the desk closer to her. A small yellow sticky slip was stuck on top of them: *I'm sorry too. Let's talk at break. Mel.*

Penny folded the note and slipped it in her purse. She looked toward Melissa, three rows away, and tried to catch her eye, but she was already working.

A small framed photograph of Robbie stood next to Penny's terminal. Penny saw Robert's chin and hair and ears. The resemblance came clearer every year.

She looked away from the eyes and down at her fingers. They were already playing across the keys, moving like confident dancers. Memories of the piano, hours and hours in grade school and junior high before she had quit it for good, welled up, the first time in years. She listened as she watched her hands, floating in front of her. She heard the piano in her mind.

CAKEWALK

NINE TEN AGAIN

The sandpile was frozen. Duck Brinweiser sat in his new '03 Ram pickup with the window down, watching Yo Ray start a fire with pieces of a tore-up pallet and a Portland cement sack. He kicked the burning wood into the culvert pipe that ran through the base of the sandpile and prodded some scrap pieces of two-by-four toward the fire with a long-handled shovel.

"Don't use that shovel in the fire, you big dummy." Ken Stick, the brick foreman, yelled out from the door of the crew trailer. "You'll ruin the temper. You want to buy Kramer a new one? They're twenty bucks apiece. Last month." He slammed the door.

"Stick the Prick," Ray said under his breath as he picked up a piece of rebar and tended the fire in the pipe. Duck listened to Ray grumble. He could almost read his mind. It would take near an hour to unthaw the sand, which meant a shorter day for the brick crew, which meant they'd be grumpy at Ray and old Henry, the other laborer-hodcarrier. And like Ray liked to say, every brickie had his head in his paycheck and his foot in some hodcarrier's business. Ray raised the rebar over his head and cracked through the ice in the 55-gallon water drum that stood between the mixer and the sand. He wound the starter rope around the mixer pulley four times.

"Give her a good one, Yo Ray," Duck yelled as he opened the door to his pickup. "First time, every time." Ray smiled and laughed as he checked the choke on the motor.

Duck's breath turned white in the early morning sun. He pulled his canvas tool bag and three-foot level out of the cab and set them on the ground. Yes, they'd be waiting on the job to get started this morning all right, but they were lucky to be getting any hours at all in late March. He hoped they could get this job closed in for inside work before cold weather fell back down on them like an icy white hammer. They'd had to lay off since early January, only coming back when the weather broke a few weeks before the bombing began overseas, and Duck's checkbook was feeling the pinch. He took the cup off his stainless steel thermos and poured. The hot coffee looked like a steaming brown tongue licking the cup.

Ray braced himself on the frozen sandy ground and pulled the starter rope hard. It snapped off the pulley with a crack, and the mixer motor turned over and gave a tired cough. Nothing more. It always took at least three good pulls. Yo Ray was usually the only one who could get the damn thing started at all though, which was one reason Stick kept him on steady.

Duck turned his back to Ray and the job site, sipping coffee and looking across the empty field west of the half-built Baptist church on the edge of Fort Scott, Kansas. The tall brown tops of dead weeds pierced a crust of snow. He felt a long way from home. He had seen Ken and the two Kramer boys, Len and Rob, go into the trailer with a bag of longjohns from Mr. Donut, and if it was like almost every other morning, they were bragging and lying to each other about last fall's hunting season. There was no sign of old Henry yet.

Ray wound and pulled the starter again. The motor still failed to catch. "I'm all fucked out," he said to nobody in particular.

Duck flinched at Ray's standard excuse. He didn't like the stream of foul language on the job. Many of the bricklayers he'd worked with couldn't say more than one

NINE TEN AGAIN

sentence without some version of the F-word in it. And the hodcarriers weren't better.

    Duck had been laying brick ten years, sometimes for himself near home around Springfield but a lot of the time on the road, anywhere in Missouri or Kansas where somebody needed help. He had worked for Kramer's outfits two or three times before, and it was okay. Stick was a decent foreman, quick to yell and just as quick to quiet down, and Kramer only came around once or twice a week, and he never filched on a paycheck, which was always a risk with a roadcrew. Duck liked working in small towns better than the winters he spent up in K.C. on big jobs. It felt more like factory work over there, even if the conditions were better, with a union steward on every job, keeping an eye out for the men. But Duck liked to be able to look into the countryside from the scaffold and still see things at least partway the way God made them.

    At his wife Mona's urging, Duck had joined the High Street Baptist congregation in Springfield four years before, and two years later he had been saved. It was one of the biggest turning points in his life, and maybe the only one he never saw coming. He always figured on graduating high school and getting married and having kids. He knew his folks would die, sooner or later. He dreamed of having a brand new pickup, and that had come to pass. But he had never figured on the feeling he had that Wednesday night in August when he accepted the Saviour over at High Street. He still couldn't talk about it much to anybody except Pastor Lewis. It was just too personal, really, just between Duck and Jesus. It was like having a best friend that you knew would never die, not ever, come hell or high water.

    Duck and Mona had two kids, Donnie and Sue, seven and ten, and every bill that came with them. Duck stayed on the road half the year. He was a good bricklayer—not the fastest, or the strongest—but steady and honest, with a good brick eye and a sense of satisfaction in a strong straight wall, both of which were valuable to any foreman. But on almost any job he felt half on the outside of everything, no matter how hard he tried to get along. This winter was no different. Duck knew Stick thought he was an oddball, too quiet to trust, but his work was good and he always showed up. He made money for Kramer and that was the point. Stick was a Baptist, too, at least in name, but his real religion was hunting. He had said more than once that he'd rather hunt than screw. Duck didn't hunt much — he took one deer each fall, mostly to fill the freezer — and the last couple of years he and Mona hadn't been been doing much in bed.

 The mixer motor caught and rumbled up. Yo Ray hauled out the hoses and hooked them together. Duck finished his coffee and squinted up at the northeast corner he'd been running all day yesterday. The corner had two-foot-wide quoin offsets both ways, a nice touch, and unusual these days — the brick corbelling in and out an inch every six courses — but it was tough to stay ahead of Len and Rob on the line and keep it plumb and pretty, the way he liked it and the way Stick ran the other corner. Twenty years from now, people would stare at Duck's corner, people who would never know his name or his long times in these weeks away from home. But it was all there anyway. That was what Duck liked about brickwork. You put yourself into it, brick by brick, and once it was there, it stayed. The name didn't matter.

 The sun rose above a wide bank of clouds spread across the eastern sky. Long shadows from the scaffold looked like the bent bars of a cage stretched over the frozen muddy ruts in the lot. Duck kicked his legs out one at a time to loosen up his muscles for the next eight hours on his feet. He felt the sun warm his back and smiled. There were worse ways to make a living.

NINE TEN AGAIN

The rest of the day seemed like a dream that turned dark and sour before Duck even knew it was happening. It was as if it wasn't real until he had time to remember it. And when he did remember it that night in the motel, he wondered if he could have seen the worst part coming.

They started up an hour late, and the brick had been ice cold all morning. Duck's fingers felt like brittle steel, and he knew everybody else's did too. Working with your hands when your hands ached like the toothache made a man mean-feeling and shortened up any temper he might be carrying around. Stick had lived up to his nickname right up to noon break, staying on Ray's back and needling Len and Rob as much as he could, considering they were the boss's boys. But Kramer and Stick went way back, and Duck figured that Kramer probably counted on Stick to be harder on his boys than he could've been himself. Over lunch, when the boys had only put about four-hundred brick into the wall between the two of them, Stick told them both that any bricklayer worth the price of his ass could lay a thousand a day, winter and summer. Rob and Len grumbled about the weather and took it out on Ray and Henry, who sat by themselves eating packed lunches.

Henry was an old drunk from St. Louis who had ended up in Fort Scott when his brother died and left him a shack in town. He was still damn good at building and stocking and tearing down scaffolding, anything where he could work off to himself. He'd worked on big jobs in St. Louis when he was younger, and he had a handy knack for keeping ahead of a crew. He was fifty and looked sixty, but most days he put out all right, and Stick counted on him to do what he was told without much lip. And that was hard to find. Most hodcarriers were liable to walk right off the job whenever they got their backs up. But Henry didn't seem to have much back left. He was white, but he put Duck in mind of an old black laborer he had worked with one winter in the city who seemed to let everything in the world roll right off and never reveal a thing about himself, month in and month out. Once in awhile Duck had wondered if he was turning out like that, too, even though he was a brickie, a notch up the ladder from any hodcarrier, no matter how they carried themselves.

About three in the afternoon the wind started in from the south, warming things up, but gritting the air real bad, too. Duck put on his dust goggles and turned over both walkboards on his corner to get rid of the mortar dust before his boots would kick it loose as he worked. The wind blew right up the wall, and the four bricklayers worked with their eyes squinted and their teeth clenched. When Rob climbed down to wash something out of his eye, Stick threw a fit.

"Your daddy doesn't pay us for washing our faces, Rob."

"Any decent job'd give it an afternoon break, Stick. If we had us a steward around, he'd shut you up quick enough."

"Maybe so, but the nearest steward's a hundred miles. Feel free to go looking for him anytime." He waved his arm toward the sky. "Anyway, I don't think you'd last on a line with them union bricklayers, boy. They'd burn you right up. They'd have you handing them their bricks and tooling up their joints. Am I right, Duck?"

Stick had a foreman's voice, one you could hear anywhere on the job, and Duck hated it when Stick tried to stir him into whatever crap was going up and down the wall. But Duck had more experience than the boys, and Stick played to that and expected Duck to play back.

"I believe you're right there, Ken. They got some real lineburners up there, for sure."

Rob was already on his way back up the scaffold.

"Hey, Kenny," Yo Ray yelled. They all knew Stick hated being called Kenny. "I need to run into town. We only have enough Portland for one batch."

"When you get to running your own jobs, then you decide who goes where when," Stick yelled, spreading a thick rope of mortar in one quick twist of his trowel.

NINE TEN AGAIN

Duck closed one eye and sighted down the length of the wall to Stick's corner at the far end. His own corner was even with Stick's, right where it should be, six courses up on the boys between. He spread mortar for another course while Stick and Ray argued on.

"Well, run out then. It don't matter a fuck to me." Ray spit at his feet.

"How many bags is there?" Stick asked.

"Two, plus a broke-open one."

Stick cut a brick in half with the edge of his trowel and trimmed it. The trowel rang against the brick like a thin bell. "Where's Henry?"

"Stocking the south scaffold."

"Have him mix a batch and be back here by the time he's done."

Rob groaned loud enough for them all to hear. Everyone knew Henry wasn't much of a mortar-man. On first sight, mixing mortar looked like something any fool with two arms and legs could do, but it was damn near an art, getting mortar right for the right job on the right day. It depended on the weather, the condition of the sand, the kind of brick. Yo Ray was a royal pain sometimes, but nine times out of ten he could keep the brickies happy with the mortar. And nothing got to a bricklayer's goat any quicker than bad mortar.

Duck had laughed to himself that afternoon, thinking of all the times he'd heard a whole line of grown men yelling at the mortar-man, "Soup-time, soup-time, send me up some crackers." Complain, complain. Sometimes they sounded like whiney kids two days after Christmas. A good bricklayer took what he got and built the best he could with it. Simple as that.

⁓

Duck sat on the motel bed beneath the velvet painting of a bullfighter, staring at the 24-hour weather channel with the sound off. The jet stream curved down behind the weatherlady's hair like a fat stripe on a half-furled flag. The afternoon kept rolling over and over in his head. He had seen and heard plenty of bad blood, or as Yo Ray would say, bad vibes, on brick jobs over the years, but nothing like this had ever happened.

Duck wished he was still a drinking man. He could use a beer tonight. Or two. Instead he pulled out the worn traveling Bible that Pastor Lewis had given him. He ran his fingers around its smooth gilded edges.

Just the touch of it calmed him down. He wondered how many people down through time had picked up a Bible to still the violent voices in their souls. But he didn't open it. What he had done that afternoon made him wonder if he should ever open it again.

∼

Henry had mixed up a terrible wet batch of mortar all right, the most common mistake somebody who didn't mix it often would make. The sand was wet from being frozen and thawed, and of course, the mud always mixed easier and quicker the wetter you made it. Stick sang out for mortar with his usual impatience and wouldn't hear of waiting to dry the batch out. Henry tied a pulley rope on a full bucket and hoisted it up to Len and Rob first, and when Rob upended the bucket, the mud slid across the board and oozed right off the scaffold, dripping onto the ground like grainy pudding.

Rob cursed Henry right off. Henry filled another bucket without saying a word. "I flat out ain't using this crap," Rob shouted. "Not till you send up a goddamn ladle to spread it with."

Stick jumped right in. "Spread for a course and let it set up while you tool out your work," he yelled. He leveled and tapped his lead corner, never looking up from his work.

Duck snapped his wooden rule out and checked his own corner against the I-beam above his head that he was working to for height. His work was just high, maybe a half-inch, which was just fine considering the way that mortar in the barrow looked.

"I'll take that next bucket, Rob," Duck said. "I can mix it in with what I still have on the board here." Duck liked Henry and he felt protective of him. He was just an old drunk, paying off a town full of people holding his bad checks.

"I told the old fart we wouldn't use it," Rob snarled up at Duck. Duck realized how much he disliked both Kramer's boys. Thank God Stick usually kept them at a distance from him.

Duck cleaned the last corbel brick joints flush with his trowel. The fresh work wasn't right yet for striking up so he started his next course of brick. He had just laid his level across it when Henry roared up the scaffold, swearing a blue streak, more words than the old man had said in a month. He pulled himself upright on the walkboards and faced off with Rob.

"I ate smart-aleck cocksuckers like you for breakfast in St. Louis. You wouldn't have this job five frigging minutes but for your old man wants to keep money in the family." Henry grabbed a short-handled mortar shovel from a bucket of water on the scaffold.

"Henry, get your soggy ass off the scaffold and put that shovel down or you won't have a job at all," Stick yelled.

Duck tapped down the high ends of two bricks and checked his level again.

Rob pointed his trowel at Henry. "Back your drunken butt off, old man, or I'll tear you a brand new one." He laughed in Henry's face.

Henry swung the shovel at Rob's trowel. Len lunged at Henry from behind and shoved him hard in the center of his back. Rob hopped out of Henry's path as the older man went down on his knees and elbows and the shovel hit the wall and clattered down to the ground.

Duck set his level down on the scaffold, watching mortar dust rise up from the three men's boots in little gray clouds. At first, it looked like that was that. Duck had been sure Stick would stop it before it went any further, and he hadn't worried about anybody falling, maybe because they weren't all that high—two jacks up, maybe fifteen feet. But Rob pulled his boot back and let the old man have one, and Henry slid right on off the inside edge of the walkboards. On the way down he banged the scaffold so hard it shook from one end to the other. For a second it felt like the whole thing might go down. They had left off every other front brace—a typical Kramer shortcut—but it stood. Duck felt sure that any able, healthy man would have at least grabbed the scaffold, but Henry seemed to have gone empty.

All four bricklayers started climbing down at once just as Yo Ray pulled onto the site in Kramer's pickup, mud spitting from the oversize back tires. Duck had been the last one to the ground, and as he thought it over that night, stretched out on the bed with the Bible in his hand, he realized that by the time he made it over to Stick and Rob and Len, they had already decided what to do next without saying a word between them.

~

In the motel room next to Duck's, a door slammed. Duck heard a woman's voice, probably Ray's latest, a barmaid at one of the local watering holes. Duck wished his room wasn't next to Ray's. Many nights he heard the two of them. Ray could bellow bad as a moose, and sometimes they would both yell swearwords and scream like there was no tomorrow.

The phone rang. Duck set his Bible on the bed.

"Hi Mona." She called every Tuesday and Thursday night like clockwork.

"No, I missed Raymond tonight," Duck answered. She sounded a long way off. "Huh, no. I fell asleep. Had a hard day." He paused. "Tough wind today. How's my family doing?"

The weather channel scrolled down a list of American cities with the day's highs and lows, followed by one-word forecasts. Duck realized how few of them he'd been to. Mona told him that Sue was upset about the TV pictures on the bombed-out house in Iraq. She said Sue had woken up with nightmares the night before.

"Don't let them watch that stuff. It'll be over soon enough. Rent some movies."

Mona sounded upset herself. She wondered if Duck had seen any of the coverage. She said they showed it over and over, so many little bodies, babies even, all charred and broken-up. She said she had never seen Sue so worked up—not even from one of those Elm Street movies she'd seen at Tina Lawson's house the year before. Duck remembered that. He'd had a long talk with Tina's father before Sue was allowed over there again.

"Let me talk to her." Duck braced himself.

"Susie? Your mother says you're having bad nightmares."

Her light high voice was a comfort to him, even with what she was talking about.

"That's way far away, honey. We just have to keep to our own faith here." She told him they were families though. Families just like their own. He wondered where she got that notion, and then he realized it didn't matter. She was right, more or less.

"I know," Duck said. "Will you come to church with me on Sunday to pray?" As he said it, he realized he hadn't been home for two weekends. Susie asked if he was working again on Saturday. It hadn't been settled yet, not with Stick, but Duck settled it in his mind right there.

"I won't, even if they ask. I promise. Hey, you love your old man?"

Duck watched his tired smile bloom in the mirror as she answered him.

"Well, he loves you, too. Can you put your mother back on a minute?"

Duck traced his index finger around the "O" of "HOLY" on the front of the book next to him. He had cracks all up and down his fingers where the lime in the mortar dried his hands up and broke them open. He wondered if he had any more Cornhusker's Lotion with him. It was the best thing he'd found for his hands.

"Mona, something pretty bad happened on the job today." Her voice rose fast on the other end. Her first worry was for Duck. Her love for him, her fears for him—they were rock bottom predictable and Duck liked that.

"No, not me. Henry Wheeling, the old laborer. He fell off the scaffold and got himself killed. I just thought you might hear something on the ten-o'clock news and worry. I'm fine. I'm okay. Hey, I told Sue I'll be home tomorrow night." He was glad he had decided. Stick was bound to ask tomorrow about working Saturday, especially with missing so much time today. Mona's voice was drifting again. Duck stared at the TV.

"I know we need the money, honey. I'm aware. Mona, let her sleep in your room if she wants, all right? God Bless."

Duck put the receiver back down. He wanted to read but his eyes hurt. He thought about all he hadn't told Mona.

∽

Among the angular shadows the scaffold cast, Henry had been absolutely still, face down with his head on a concrete block, blood dripping over both sides of the block. As Duck walked up behind the Kramer boys, Stick pulled his hand away from Henry's throat.

"He's dead," Stick said, looking up at the walkboards above their head.

NINE TEN AGAIN

The four of them stood beneath the scaffold. Rob was shaking. He reached down toward Henry's body. Stick stopped him.

"Don't turn him over. Not unless you're fond of nightmares, boy."

Duck called for Jesus in his mind. Yo Ray left the pickup running and came running toward the scaffold.

"What happened?" he yelled. He had a Big Gulp soft drink in his hand.

"Henry fell off the scaffold," Stick said. He looked through the arched opening in the wall opposite them. Inside the unfinished church, two sparrows flew by.

"It's a terrible thing," Stick said. He squared around to face them all. He didn't look at Len and Rob. He avoided Yo Ray's eye and settled into a calm stare right at Duck. "A terrible accident. The old man stumbled and just didn't have enough gas to even try to catch himself."

Everybody but Duck and Stick stared hard at the dead man's back. The pickup died and dieseled. The sparrows made noise from the other side of the wall.

Yo Ray threw the Big Gulp at the wall. Ice cubes clinked like glass on the brick.

"Jesus H. Christ," he yelled. "Poor screwed-up old fart. I never seen anybody die on the job before." It looked like he might cry—his big face crumpled up, his bushy eyebrows and his sideburns and his beard all coming together. "I never did."

"I seen it once," Stick said. "It ain't a cakewalk out here. Never has been. Right, Duck?"

Duck felt the wind dry the glistening around his own eyes. He gazed up at the walls and the scaffold. The mortar in the barrow was setting up fast now.

"Duck?" Stick asked him again, directly. He turned his head and looked over at Duck's pickup in a way that made Duck look, too—the paintjob still perfect, the whitewalls still clean, a sheet of 3/4 inch plywood protecting the bed, the Support Our Troops ribbon decal centered on the bright chrome bumper. Stick's eyes came back to the church, waiting for Duck's answer.

"No, it's no cakewalk, Ken," Duck said. It was his own voice. He hadn't heard any other.

Stick looked at Duck and nodded. Then he took charge.

"Go to the trailer, Ray, and call the police. Tell them we have a dead worker out here. Then clean up the mixer and dump this barrow in those deep ruts by the trailer. Cover that sandpile with the tarp. We'll call it for today, but I want to get an early start tomorrow—the carpenters are breathing down my neck. They want to set roof joists by early next week. Len, you and Rob get your tools and clear out for the day. Me and Duck will strike her up."

When everybody began moving, Duck walked to his pickup and pulled his wallet out of the glove compartment. He looked at his pictures in their plastic sleeves. Mona, five years ago, before she changed her hair color. Sue, last year at the end of fifth grade, her smile simple as sunshine. And Donnie, in his cubscout uniform and new glasses.

He turned back to the job. Stick had covered Henry up with a piece of ragged green tarp. When the Kramer boys pulled their pickup out on the highway, they didn't look at Duck. Stick started striking up the wall like it was any other day.

"Duck. Give me a hand here," he yelled.

Duck walked slowly back to the scaffold and climbed up. The joints were setting fast. He pressed his joiner against the bricks as hard as he could, taking comfort in the sound of the cold steel racing across the hard sandy surfaces, smoothing and sealing each joint in the wall.

⁓

When he heard noises in the next room, Duck was sitting up but only half-awake, right at the edge of real dreaming. He could still see old Henry, loaded like a side of beef into the ambulance van, leaving a brick job for the last time, riding to Crosby's Funeral Home on a windy winter afternoon. The ambulance roared onto the site with its siren wailing, but when it left you could hear the gravel under its tires as clear as bone breaking bit by bit. The police took short statements from Stick and Duck and then were gone ten minutes after the ambulance left. The last thing Duck noticed when he left was that the bloody concrete block under the scaffold hadn't been moved. Somebody would have to do that in the morning.

Yo Ray bellowed twice from the next room. The weather channel showed an updated forecast map for the weather where the troops were.

Duck set his Bible on the nightstand. He draped his pants and T-shirt over a chair and turned the TV off. He watched the tiny point of light in the center of the screen shrink to nothing. Even after it was gone, he stared at where it had been.

PRESIDENT OF SOMETHING

NINE TEN AGAIN

The afternoon snow had ended. Lyle turned into his driveway and stopped, facing the front of his motorhome. He looked at the four videos and VCR on the seat next to him and glanced at the time readout on the dash. Joanne and the kids would be home any minute.

From under the seat, Lyle pulled out the movie he'd rented from the X-rated room at the back of United Video after the family had left. Only a title, *Intrigues*, and a running time, forty-nine minutes. Lyle didn't remember much about the only other such movies he had seen, almost twenty years before in college, except that the scenes were shadowy and indistinct, not unlike the mix of guilt and mild excitement he felt now, remembering them, as well as guessing at the gist of *Intrigues*. He slipped the movie back under the seat, and stared through his windshield at the motorhome. The chrome logo above the front bumper read *Open Road*. The blue letters of the customized license plate spelled out *FAMLEVAN*.

Any Saturday afternoon in mid-winter was a restless time around the house for Lyle, and this one seemed worse, with heavy snow starting around noon, and the coverage of the bombing overseas, incessant on the TV news channels. Everyone seemed to think it was a good idea when Lyle suggested they go out and rent a movie. Joanne had shopping to do, so she and Tracy, the baby of the family, drove in the new '90 Toyota. Lyle and Jason, the fifteen-year-old, took the older car, an '84 VW.

Jason was "stoked," as he put it, about soon getting his learner's permit, and it showed every time he rode in the car. He was counting the days until his half-birthday, less than two months away, and he'd already memorized the state regulation booklet, cover to cover. On the way to the mall he watched Lyle's every move, catching him once as he swung into the right lane on a wide left turn. The rest of the way down Hillview, Lyle drove slower than usual, trying to model his best defensive driving. He hesitated so much for one stale green light that a truck horn blared and Jason laughed. Lyle was relieved when they parked at the mall.

"*Red Dawn*," Jason said, once the four of them gathered in front of the store.

"How many times have you seen that?" Lyle didn't wait for an answer. "And no war movies, not today," Lyle said. "I had a family film in mind." He couldn't place the four of them watching a movie together in months.

"What's a big deal with today?" Jason asked.

"People are dying?" Lyle said. "Big enough?"

"You're not dying. I'm not dying."

"Our pilots could be," Lyle said. Jason was at the age where it was difficult, and important, not to let him get the last word.

"Ly—le, we're only renting movies here," Joanne said.

"That's what soldiers do," Jason said.

"*My Time on the Mountain?*" Joanne suggested. "Tracy honey, would you like it? It's about a brave woman who hurts herself skiing."

"No way, Mom, it's a dumb movie," Jason said. "Let's all pick our own."

"No matter how much pain she's in, she never complains," Joanne said.

"*Pound Puppies*," Tracy said. She looked up from the shoelaces she was trying to tie.

Lyle winced. He'd sat through it twice with her. "I give up. Maybe you're right, Jace."

"Fine," Joanne said. "We never tried that." She grinned like she was telling a joke. "If you count the little one in the motorhome, we do have four TV's."

Lyle frowned. He knew she knew it wasn't what he wanted.

"VCR's are cheap to rent," she said, building on an argument Lyle believed she had no real stake in. "They're not much more than an extra movie."

"That's your idea of togetherness?" Lyle asked.

"We'll make popcorn together," Joanne said, "we're together right now. Let's each pick out our own movie and then get cones at B & R before Tracy and Jason and I go shopping."

"I want Rocky Road," Tracy said. "In a sugar cone."

"Double chocolate fudge brownie," Jason said.

Lyle stared at the cardboard stand-up in the video store window. An oversize gun barrel pointed out at him, held in the hand of a muscular man with no shirt. A redhead in a short vinyl skirt and stiletto heels raised one leg high around the man's waist. Lyle thought of his ex-brother-in-law, Ed, telling him about the movies he and Joanne's sister watched, ones where they showed absolutely everything. Lyle saw the neon X at the back of the store. He looked at Joanne. He didn't think she'd ever seen a movie like that.

"What kind of ice cream do you want?" he asked her.

∼

They ate popcorn from two big bowls, one with salt for Joanne and Jason, one without for Lyle and Tracy. Jason showed off his new sports shoes, and Joanne talked about the towels she'd found at forty per cent off. Tracy wiped butter on her shoelaces. When Joanne asked what movie Lyle had settled on, he showed them *The Verdict*. It was a courtroom drama he'd wanted to see years before but missed.

"Bore-ing," Jason said, his hand tapping his open mouth in a mock yawn.

Lyle turned to him. "Serious doesn't have to be boring."

"Whatever," Jason said. He held up the stainless steel bowl in his lap like a greasy concave mirror. "Nothing but old maids," he said. "Must be movie time."

"Don't call them that," Joanne said, looking at Lyle, who'd been the source of the expression years back. "We don't use that phrase." She smiled and raised her eyebrows. "So honey, who's getting stuck in the motorhome?"

Lyle didn't answer. He watched Jason spin the empty bowl on his finger.

"I'll get Tracy started on hers," Joanne said. "You sure you don't want to watch *Pretty Woman* with me, Lyle? Julia Roberts plays a beautiful call girl." Joanne started to laugh, as if Lyle's attraction to women in the movies was a leftover teenage quirk she still found amusing.

"And Gere plays a rich executive," Lyle said. He knew Joanne had seen it at least once before, and he had the sense that Gere fascinated Joanne. He wondered how often they saw different movies even when they watched the same one.

Now Joanne didn't answer. "All right," Lyle said, "I'll take the motorhome." He thought of his movie under the car seat. "Great way for a family to spend Saturday night."

"An experiment," Joanne said. "It's no worse than three of us watching something we don't like."

"I tied it," Tracy yelled. She beamed at the bow on her shoe.

"That's good," Lyle said. He leaned over and picked her up. She sat in his lap, holding her shoe like a trophy.

"See, everything's fine," Joanne said. "Our baby's tying her shoes, and we have brand new towels and four good movies." She laughed a full laugh then, one that ended with a slight smiling trill, a sound and sight that Lyle loved, that he had always believed would do for grace until the real thing came along. "We can enjoy Saturday night our own way," she said. "Nobody's keeping track. There's nobody for us to impress."

Lyle smiled back, staring past her. It was true. Who cared what went on in their house? It was only the four of them, separated off under one roof, like every other family up and down the block, up and down all the blocks. And they were free inside their houses, inside their families. But free for what?

"Lyle? You with us?"

"Huh? Yeah, I'm fine. We don't have to impress anybody."

"That's what I just said."

Tracy was sitting on the floor again. Jason had taken his movie up to his room. Lyle picked up the shiny empty popcorn bowls.

"I heard you," he said.

～

Lyle turned on the portable heater in the *Open Road* and hooked up the VCR before he went back to check on Tracy. She lay on the living room floor, engrossed in *Prancer*, already looking sleepy. Jets in *Top Gun* roared so loudly in Jason's room that Lyle heard them from downstairs. He went up to the master bedroom and stood in the door.

"Isn't that bothering you?" he asked Joanne, pointing down the hall.

She lay on the bed across the room. She put a finger to her lips. "It's all right. Just close the door," she said. "I don't want to miss the beginning."

On the way back Lyle retrieved the other movie from the car. Alone in the motorhome he heard himself think that Joanne had wanted him to make his own choice and that this served her right. It was a small feeling, but Lyle tried to savor it. He put *The Verdict* on first, as if someone might be keeping tabs, but after a few minutes he switched movies.

He turned the sound off and locked the door first.

Ed was right. Though the action looked staged, it was brightly lit and it did show everything. Lyle felt himself stiffen, and he imagined going up to the bedroom and stripping in front of Joanne without a word of explanation. But it seemed dishonest, like thinking of another woman while they made love, something he tried not to do, although she had never accused him of it. He pressed *STOP* and closed his eyes. He would take the damned movie back and forget it ever happened. It wasn't a big deal, as much boredom as anything else. The voice he heard was his and not his, a voice that usually gave others, and occasionally Lyle himself, the benefit of the doubt. In the midst of the voices, someone knocked on the door.

Lyle opened his eyes. News flickered on the TV. He stood up and clicked the overhead light on. The door rattled and he heard a louder knock. "A minute," he yelled. He shoved both *The Verdict* and the empty case for *Intrigues* under a seat cushion before he opened the door.

"Why's the door locked?" Jason asked. He stepped into the motorhome.

"I didn't know it was," Lyle said. "I was half asleep."

"Told you it was a boring movie," Jason said. "Here." He handed Lyle a beer. "Mom said to bring it. I think she's feeling guilty."

"Thanks." Lyle sipped the beer. "How's *Top Gun*?"

"Same as always," Jason said, "great. I paused it." He looked at the TV. A commentator stood in front of a map of some part of the Middle East. Or Eastern Europe. Lyle wasn't sure at first glance. Jason looked back at Lyle. "Dad, what would you say if I joined the Air Force?"

"I'd say you're too young."

"I don't mean now. When I'm eighteen."

"Well, when you're eighteen, let's talk. I can tell you right now though, there are much better ways to pay for college, Jason." As Lyle said it though, he realized that if

Jason did join the service, it could save tens of thousands of dollars, could save Lyle thousands of tedious hours at the office running numbers through underwriting programs.

Lyle had never imagined his son in the service before, but he saw that it was only one of a flood of possiblities he hadn't considered, ones that didn't fit his picture of the future. The future he always expected was dwarfed in comparison, as tenuous as a spit of beach sand between wide waters at high tide. His son might join the Air Force and disappear behind a Tom Cruise grin. Lyle or Joanne themselves might turn from the bedroom mirror one night and peel away the promises of their marriage like layers from a make-up mask. It could even happen all in one horrid evening, like in that old movie with Burton and Taylor at each others' throats.

"I wasn't thinking about college," Jason said. "I was thinking about women."

"Women?" Lyle said. He tasted popcorn in the back of his throat.

"You know," Jason said, "girls. None of them look twice at me now." He paused. "It's almost all I ever think about, Dad."

"There's nothing wrong with that," Lyle said.

"Sometimes I hate it," Jason said. "Sometimes I hate them."

It was more than he'd ever said about what he was going through, but Lyle couldn't respond. He remembered their serious facts-of-life talks years before. Those had seemed easy. Jason was only curious and a little embarrassed and completely amazed. But now he'd wandered into territory Lyle could only vaguely remember, an intense country of urges and disappointments that Lyle had somehow found his own way through without ever really understanding. Jason walked toward the door.

"Every young man feels confused at your age," Lyle said.

"That doesn't help," Jason said. His grin looked as lame

as Lyle's felt, yet Lyle knew he was pleased to be called a man, even if indirectly. Jason stepped back and sat down at the table.

"What's this?" He leaned forward and pulled the two movie cases from under the cushion.

"*The Verdict*," Lyle said.

"There's two here." Jason stared at the empty video case.

"It's just an extra," Lyle said. "Why don't you go finish your movie now?"

Jason stared from Lyle to the TV. He reached out and punched the *PLAY* button before Lyle could react. The *PLAY* sign flashed above a beer commercial, and then a different image filled the screen, a brunette on a bed, leaning on her elbows. Jason's eyes flared. "Damn," he said. He turned the volume up, and the woman moaned in a falsetto voice. Lyle grabbed Jason's arm and pulled him out of the booth and onto the floor. He clicked both the VCR and TV off.

"That's your movie?" Jason said from the floor. Lyle stood over him, his jaw grinding. He helped Jason up.

"It's not my movie. I took it on a whim. I've never rented one before."

"I'll bet," Jason said. "And you wanted a family movie."

"You and your mother outvoted me, remember?" Lyle couldn't believe he was spouting the same weak excuse to his son that he'd been hearing in his own head.

"What would she think?" Jason asked. He moved his eyes in the direction of the closed blinds on the window and the house beyond them.

"Forget you saw it," Lyle said. "It's fake anyway. They're only going through motions."

Jason pointed at the window. "Like you and her?"

Lyle raised his hand before he could think. Inches from Jason's face he pulled back his fist. "You don't know anything," he said. "You're just a kid. Get out of here."

Jason's hands shook and he looked at the floor. "Sorry,"

he said. "It was just a joke."

Lyle didn't believe that was all there was to it, but if he was right, he didn't want to know more. "Not a funny one," he said.

"I can tell." Jason rubbed his jaw as if he were imagining how the blow might have felt. But then he raised his face slowly and looked Lyle directly in the eye. It shocked Lyle. The two of them were the same height.

"I want to watch it," Jason said.

"Well, you can't. Look Jason, I made a mistake. It has nothing to do with the real me. Or your mother."

Jason stepped out of Lyle's reach. His eyes glinted. "I could tell her."

"Why in the world are you talking this way?" Lyle asked. He felt his stomach knot as if someone had punched him. "You can't watch it, and you won't tell your mother. I know you better than that." Lyle ejected the movie and put it in the case. "It's over," he said. "It's on its way out of here. And so are we. Let's go."

On the way to the house Lyle put the movie back under the front seat and locked the car. At the door he stopped Jason.

"You won't tell your mother." He said it as a statement, but in his mind it was a question.

"I'd like to see her if she knew the truth," Jason said.

"There's no truth to it," Lyle said. "It's just a stupid dirty movie. The world's full of them. I'm sure you'll see them sooner or later." Lyle put his hand on the doorknob.

"Maybe in the Air Force," Jason said as he turned away.

The last word again. Lyle tried to ignore it, to let him have it this time. They stood on the familiar front porch, the same one the two of them had painted together just the previous summer.

"I won't tell her," Jason said. He walked in as Lyle held the door. "And you won't either."

When Lyle walked into the darkened master bedroom, Gere and Roberts were making love in dim light on thick carpet. Joanne lay in bed with the room lights out and the covers pulled up. She turned toward Lyle but then averted her eyes, as if he had walked in on the movie at either the worst or the best moment, Lyle wasn't sure which. They both watched the scene end, the music overpowering the sounds of the stars' lovemaking as the camera panned in for a close-up of their faces. Even near the height of pleasure, Gere's character seemed confident and nonchalant.

"I guess I see why you wanted this movie," Lyle said. His hypocrisy had to be as visible as a rash, but he felt he had to speak first.

"It's not all like that," Joanne said. "It's a nice story. Is yours over already?"

"Jason was right." He pointed down the hall where the navy jets roared again. "It was boring."

"Want to watch the rest of this one?" she asked. "I can catch you up on the plot pretty quick." She pulled back the covers and patted the bed. She wore only her robe.

Lyle undressed and hung his shirt and pants over the chair beside the door and closed it. He walked to the bed. Joanne opened her arms, and her robe. Lyle climbed into bed and pulled the sheets up behind himself, covering both of them completely.

By the time Lyle felt the room rising back around him, the movie was over. The late news recapped the latest briefings about the air raids. There was little resistance anywhere.

Joanne pressed the *REWIND* and turned the TV off. She went down to check on Tracy in her bed. When she came back upstairs, Lyle heard her knock on Jason's door, but there was no answer. The house was quiet.

"Jason's already asleep, too," she said, slipping under the covers again.

NINE TEN AGAIN

"Joanne, there's something I want to tell you."

"Well, tell me quick," she said. "You made me sleepy." She smiled and yawned.

Lyle looked from her smile to the ceiling, unable to speak. Jason was right.

"Jason asked me what I'd think if he joined the Air Force."

"Our Jason? In the Air Force?" She shook her head. "What'd you say?"

"I told him we'd talk when he was old enough."

"That was good," she said. "There's no sense giving him a wall to bang his head against. He'll forget all about it next week." She stretched and yawned again.

Lyle wasn't so sure. He stared at the blank screen, the various versions of the future he had glimpsed in the motorhome running across it like previews for confusing films, all with the same familiar characters. "What was the name of that old Burton and Taylor movie?" he asked. "The one with all the screaming and handwringing?" He turned to Joanne. Her eyes had closed.

Lyle picked up the remote and surfed the channels on *MUTE*. He watched a simulated bombing mission unfold in silence—intricate dials and meters against the pale blue world beyond the cockpit, and then a precise line of puffs on the ground below, off-white flowers popping into bloom one after the other. He turned it off.

When he went to the bathroom, light flickered under Jason's door and Lyle heard a low moaning. He walked back to his own room and checked his pants. The car keys were gone.

~

Lyle sat behind the wheel of the cold motorhome in his robe and parka and lined slippers. He imagined himself on one of the family's long summer trips, late at night in unfamiliar country. Driving the *Open Road*, especially at night, usually made him alert with a vigilance he enjoyed, as if he were a pilot or president of something, responsible for everything, his wife napping beside him, his children asleep above his head.

A little after eleven he heard the front door of the house opening. He didn't know what he would say, but he was determined to make sure the boy knew he hadn't gotten away with it. Jason hurried down the front steps in jeans and a T-shirt. He wore no socks and the laces on his new shoes trailed in the snow. He didn't see Lyle as he unlocked the driver's door of the VW, but when he reached down to put the movie beneath the seat, Lyle started the motorhome.

Jason jumped back and froze, staring up at Lyle. Then he sat down behind the steering wheel and started the car, too. Neither of them moved.

Lyle watched the car's cold exhaust rise into the night like a frayed white rope. He stared at Jason's face through the two windshields, but he lost his eyes among the reflections of the night sky and his own face. It occurred to him that Jason could back the car out of the driveway and disappear down the street. He tried to picture the two of them swerving through lanes of traffic, like all the flight and pursuit scenes in the movies. He glanced at the dash. All the gauges looked good, the gas full, the oil pressure normal, the alternator charging like it should.

After another minute the rope of exhaust disappeared. Jason stepped out and clicked the car door shut. He walked toward the house. Lyle rolled down his window and called to him.

Jason turned around. "I'm cold. You gonna take another swing at me?"

"I didn't swing. I thought about it, but I didn't. I want to talk."

Jason walked closer. "What's there to say?"

"I want to help you through this."

"Through what? The tough years?" Jason's tone said he had heard it all before. Lyle vowed to himself it wouldn't be that way tonight.

"Whatever you want to name it. Girls. Sex. Life."

"Can you?"

"I'm not sure." Lyle looked to the street and back.

Jason shrugged and looked at the street, too. He didn't say anything for awhile, and when he did, his sarcasm was gone. "Are you and Mom happy?"

"Yes." It was too simple to be the whole truth, but it wasn't a lie.

"Then why'd you get that movie?" Jason waved his hand at the car.

"Jace, we do things every day, sometimes all day long, that we don't always have the why's for. You have to accept that. With yourself as well as other people."

"I couldn't quit watching it," Jason said.

Lyle tried to imagine his son in his dark bedroom, isolated in sexual desperation, but all that came were his own memories of nights he had spent alone at the same age, his room vibrant with phantom women. Lyle stretched his arm out the window, his fingers grazing Jason's shirt. "I want to be honest to each other."

"It's hard to be honest," Jason said.

Lyle turned the motorhome engine off. It was very quiet in the neighborhood.

"You didn't tell her, did you?" Jason asked.

Lyle shook his head no, giving Jason his chance to say I told you so. Jason didn't speak.

"But I may yet. Your mother's unpredictable. You have to know that by now. And pretty wise. She might laugh it off, or she could be hurt." Lyle paused. "Who knows? She might even want to see it."

Jason's eyes widened. This wasn't anything he'd heard before, at least that much was certain. He shifted his weight and shivered. He pointed at the car.

"I almost took off just now," he said. "I could drive it."

"I know you could," Lyle said. He held out his hand with the palm up.

Jason put the keys in Lyle's hand and turned and walked up the steps into the house. Lyle listened to the ticks and snaps of the engine and stared through the windshield at the tops of bare maple and birch trees behind the house. Somewhere overhead, above the cloud cover, a jet rumbled across the sky. Lyle knew it was only a commercial plane, full of travelers and people like himself, but still, he had a vision of his house exploding in a gray puff of smoke.

He put his hands on the wheel and gripped it hard. He forced himself to take slow breaths, until it all settled back down in front of him, piece by piece. The foundation, floors, walls, and roof. And then person by person. Joanne, Tracy, Jason, Lyle.

The rumble of the plane faded. Lyle relaxed his hands and imagined the house from above, whole and undisturbed now, receding steadily into the shadowy patterns of the blocks, the neighborhoods, the city, and then the mountains all around.

LEANING

NINE TEN AGAIN

Dee and the other cheerleaders went through their routine moves while the announcer introduced the players. The Grizzlies had won the league the year before in '89-90, and they had a good shot again this year, already leading by two games in the middle of January. ESPN was broadcasting the game live—the first time ever for a home game in Missoula—and for a moment Dee let herself imagine cheerleading at the spring NCAA regionals.

Just as her squad finished their sequence, a dozen students ran onto the court and fell down on the polished hardwood. They scattered across the floor, stretching from one free throw line to the other. They wore identical white T-shirts with *Play Ball Not War* printed in black letters both front and back.

"What are they doing?" Dee yelled at Leanne, the closest cheerleader, her roommate, and Dee wanted to believe, her best friend, although Leanne had many other friends. Leanne, a junior, had helped Dee make the varsity cut by telling her what to say in the interview and showing her special moves for the tryout. The two of them shared a cramped room in Jesse Hall, but Dee liked it better than the single room she'd lived in during her freshman year.

Leanne rolled her eyes. "A protest," she said. "The war thing."

While the crowd jeered at the protestors, the cheerleaders huddled. Then all six of them lined up and waved twelve purple and white pom-poms, trying to distract the fans, and the ESPN cameramen, with one of their standard cheers. The crowd joined in and quickly converted the cheer to their own chant: "Saddam Sucks, Saddam Sucks." The protestors lay still on the hardwood. An apple shattered on the court near one of them, its brittle seeds skittering across the shiny floor. From high up in the stands, popcorn rained down like hollow yellow hail.

 Dee kicked her legs high and waved her arms and leaned backwards and then forwards in the way she'd been taught, but when Leanne gave up and turned around to watch, she did too. Dee had never seen a war protest, or really, a protest of anything, except on TV. As security guards and a few fans grappled with the limp bodies, Dee noticed the lone woman protestor. Besides the T-shirt with the slogan, she wore faded blue jeans and aqua hightop tennis shoes. Dee recognized her from an American history class a year before. Two uniformed men grabbed the woman's belt loops and pulled her across the slick floor. Her eyes were closed. Right in front of the cheerleaders, one of her belt loops broke. The guards stopped and readjusted their grip, grabbing her under the shoulders. The woman's eyes opened and she stared directly at Dee.

 Dee stared back. She tried to picture herself lying on the floor with thousands of people screaming at her, but instead she saw what she believed the woman on the floor must see, an imposter, a fake girl, standing in a pleated skirt and lettered sweater, a pom-pom dangling from each hand.

 The guards started sliding the woman again, along with several others, on their way to the south arena entrance. A student right behind Dee at courtside stood up and yelled and pointed at the girl. "Go die somewhere else." Dee pivoted and reached up and slapped at his face. Her palm grazed off his beard as he pulled back.

 "What the hell?" he screamed. The noise in the field house drowned his voice.

"I'm sorry," she yelled. She didn't remember ever trying to hit anyone in her life, not even her father.

The young man glared at her as he moved away with the throng that surged behind the protestors into the concourse. As Dee watched him go, she saw Louis, the guy she was going out with after the game, standing in the bleachers, his slate-gray eyes focused on her. Dee wondered if he had seen her try to hit the bearded man. Two students stood up in front of him and blocked her view.

A loudspeaker crackled as fans hauled the last protestor off the court. Team assistants began brooming off and wiping down the playing surface. The announcer's voice reassured the crowd. The game would begin in only a few more minutes.

The Grizzlies won. Dee tried to forget her confusion during the protest and the eyes of the woman on the floor, and the win helped her do that. Plus she had the date with Louis, their fourth date. She hurried back to her room with Leanne after the game and changed clothes.

"You two serious?" Leanne asked, pulling on her white jeans, dressing for a night with Sandy, a senior business major. They were engaged.

"I like him. I don't really know him that well."

"Who's he gone out with?"

"I haven't asked."

"Where's he from?"

"He's out-of-state. Near Denver, I think. We met at a party. He's in Pharmacy so we don't have classes in the same building." Dee was a pre-accounting major. Although she didn't really like numbers, she'd always been naturally quick with them, and her advisor had steered her to the Business School.

"Must be some kind of brain." Leanne opened a built-in

drawer on her side of the bureau. "He has a great body, too." She pulled two condoms in pastel wrappers out of a box in the drawer. Rose and lilac.

Dee looked away. "You noticed. I guess it's good you're taken."

"Does he play a sport?" Leanne asked. She put the condoms in her purse and then looked at Dee. "Did you want one of those?"

Leanne seemed to like to shock Dee just enough so she could reassure her. Though Dee was really two months older, Leanne treated her like a younger sister, and Dee tried to act like one, even going as far as lying to Leanne on her birthday, subtracting a year to be the right age for her class. Despite that it had been ten years before, Dee was ashamed she'd repeated a grade. It had been the fourth grade, a blank numb year when Dee felt too timid and exhausted to get out of bed for school and the doctors couldn't say why. Now all that remained of that year was an extra number on her age she couldn't explain. It was easier to delete it.

"I think he just works out." Dee pointed at Leanne's purse. "Doesn't Sandy get those?"

"If I banked on that, I'd be pregnant already. No thank you."

"You don't think it should be up to the guy?"

"My small-town girl," Leanne said, "you little Marionette." Leanne often teased Dee about her tiny high school in Chinook, especially about the name for the cheerleading squad there. Sometimes Dee wished she'd never told Leanne that, and yet without that certain style of kidding between them, Dee wasn't sure they would have become friends, or roommates, in the first place. Leanne was the one who had nicknamed her, too, at the end of her freshman year, and now everyone but her parents, certainly everyone she knew on campus, called her Dee. She liked it. She had secretly craved the nickname—it was so much less formal and distant than Deirdre— but a nickname wasn't something you gave yourself.

"That's probably why I get such a kick out of you," Leanne said.

Dee smiled, standing in her bra and underwear, goose bumps on her shoulders and hips.

"If you go dressed like that, you better take the rest of the box," Leanne added, pointing back to the drawer. She laughed. "Just kid-ding." She opened the door. "See you." Dee heard two women yell at each other somewhere down the hall.

"Will you be gone all night?" Dee asked.

"With luck," Leanne said. She pulled the door shut as she spoke.

Dee pulled the condom box out of Leanne's drawer. They were a different brand than she and her only steady boyfriend had used. Dee tried to picture Jeremy, her high-school boyfriend, a long-distance runner who had started college with her but dropped out to work on his dad's ranch on Lodge Creek. In her remembrance at least, he lacked some essential dimension—depth, maybe, or something like depth—and Dee feared the lack was her fault. Her memories of him were flat and paper-thin, like midday reflections on the surface of a lake.

On the box, a couple in bathing suits embraced on a beach. The woman tossed her head back as the man kissed her shoulder. Each package had the words *Machine Tested* printed on it.

Dee put the box in her purse and slung the purse strap over her shoulder, trying to feel nonchalant, but in the mirror, she looked awkward and vulnerable. Whenever Leanne left, Dee felt uneasy in the tiny room in the tall building. She thought of those stupid old college movies, *Animal House* or *Revenge of the Nerds*, where boys drilled holes in the walls or climbed ladders to peek in windows. She was glad she was on Fourth. Nobody would find a ladder that tall.

She walked to the window and looked out on the lights of Missoula, but she could see her reflection there, too, shifting in the glass as she moved. It was a feeling she often had, as if somebody familiar was following her, watching to find a weakness in the smallest details—the way she held her face in the mirror or how she moved her hands when she wrote in her diary.

Dee took the box out of her purse and put it back in Leanne's drawer. She finished dressing. The hamper hinge rasped as she opened it and threw her cheerleader's skirt and sweater in. As she closed the door to the room, her pom-poms on the bed reminded her of the stuffed animals she had left behind at home.

―

"It was scary," Dee said to Louis when he mentioned the outburst in the field house. They were parked on a South Hills cul-de-sac that overlooked the city, the street paved but without houses yet, only orange wooden stakes and stiff knapweed stalks poking through snow. Dee could make out her dorm building rising in the distance like a square modern castle. Less than half the room lights were on. It was after midnight.

"A die-in. Now there's a stupid pet trick," Louis said. He handed her another wine cooler and put his arm around her. She remembered several coolers at the party for the team at a frat house on Connell Street, and Louis had bought more afterwards. She let him slide her closer.

"Cameras," he said, "that's what they did it for. They're just jealous of the troops."

"Would you go?" Dee wasn't sure why she asked him.

"To the Mid-East? You crazy? I'm going to be a pharmacist."

His honesty surprised her. She thought of her brother Grady. She was glad he was still in high school.

"Well, at least we won the game," Louis said. "If we'd lost on top of that sideshow, it would have been serious down-time." His hand rested on her knee.

Dee liked the way Louis used expressions nobody else she knew would. Yet she couldn't relax with the way he approached her. The first time he'd taken her back to the dorm, he kissed her cheek, a light friendly kiss—the way Dee always hoped her father might kiss her—but then he had put his hand on her breast, heavily, without moving, as if his hand or her breast, or both, were made of stone. Yet except for that one moment, Louis had behaved as if sex was the last thing on his mind.

He kissed her now though, and she ran her hand across his chest. The car radio played *From a Distance*. One of them kicked over an empty wine cooler on the floor. Louis kept pressing onto her as she slowly leaned back across the car seat. Dee thought of what Leanne said about the condoms. Louis kept his mouth closed, and Dee wondered if he was shy. She pressed her tongue against his lips. He pulled back.

"I know what you want," he said. In what seemed like one fluid motion he lifted her up from beneath her coat and dress and pulled her panties to her knees. It reminded her of the way her father skinned rabbits he brought home to dress out. He said the trick was to do it in one quick motion without any hesitation.

"What are you doing?" Dee sat up, feeling sober all at once, as quickly as the time a sheriff had shined a flashlight in on her and Jeremy on a ranch lane outside of Chinook.

"I want it, too," he said. "I was wild watching your moves at the game tonight." He stretched his legs out straight and unzipped his pants.

Dee forced away from him and sat upright, pushing her skirt down with both hands.

"No," she said, "no." She knew she was in the right, but she didn't want to make Louis dislike her either.

He stopped, his hand still on his zipper. He turned his face away from her. "How about a hand-job then?"

"What?" Dee felt her face contort, like a mask she was trying to wriggle out of. Anger made her feel fake and unattached to her own body.

Louis looked at her and then zipped his pants back up. He gripped the wheel and glared straight ahead then, his knuckles white and his jaw flexing.

"I'm sorry," he said, "I really like you, Dee."

"Why would you talk that way then?"

"I thought you were teasing me." He turned the heater back up and reached for the gear shift but paused before he pulled around the cul-de-sac. "Maybe we had too much cooler." He pointed at the empty bottles on the floorboards.

They didn't speak again until they were near the dorm. On the way Louis stretched his open hand out on the seat between them. As they pulled into the parking lot, Dee rested her palm on his. She tried to forget what he'd said and the metallic slide of his zipper.

"Your light's out," Louis said.

"How can you tell?" Dee asked, looking up at the building.

"You're the one on the end, there, aren't you? On Fourth?"

"How did you know which one?"

"You told me, didn't you? Isn't Leanne home? I'm glad we got a chance to hang out with her and Sandy at the party. She's a neat girl."

"She's staying with him tonight. Yeah, she's the closest thing I have to a best friend." Dee thought back. She couldn't remember ever showing him which room was hers.

"That's a great thing to have. Can I walk you to the door?"

Two yellow ribbons hung from each of the front door handles. Louis took Dee's hand as they walked into the lobby. Dee said hello to the R.A. behind the desk across the room.

NINE TEN AGAIN

He wore walkman headphones and his head bobbed up and down. He didn't look up as they walked past. He was drawing fat pink lines across the pages of a psychology textbook.

～

In the dorm room Dee undressed and put on Leanne's robe that hung from the hook on the inside of the double closet. Dee had her own robe, but not one that soft, and Leanne's felt good against her skin. She sat down at the corner desk to write in her diary, trying to make herself sleepy. She turned off all the lights but the reading lamp on the wall above the desk. It cast a narrow cone of light on the page and her hands. She wrote about the team winning the game and the fun the four of them had at the party. She remembered the song her mother liked to sing around the house when she cleaned. *Accent-U-Ate The Positive.*

When she felt sleepy enough, she snapped the light off. She thought about slipping into bed in Leanne's robe, but she had her own pajamas hanging on her side of the closet. She was just hanging Leanne's robe back in its place when she heard voices outside the door. She froze in the darkness, naked, listening.

It was Leanne and Sandy. Both their voices were slowed and slurred. There was a key working in the lock. Before Dee knew what she was doing, she stepped into the closet and pulled both doors closed behind her. She heard laughter from the hall.

"Can't you fit that thing in the slot," Leanne said.

"Don't you worry about that," Sandy said. The key and the lock kept jiggling.

"You're going to wake her up," Leanne said.

"Which way does it turn?"

"Just keep moving it back and forth," Leanne said. She was laughing again.

The door opened. Dee sensed light through the cracks

around the hinges of the closet, and Leanne and Sandy's voices and laughter were louder and closer. Dee leaned further back into the corner of the closet. Suddenly there was even more light.

"Don't turn the light on, you cretin—"

"There's nobody here but you and me, Annie."

"Dee? Are you here? Dee?"

"Is she in the bathroom?"

Leanne knocked on the partly closed bathroom door. "I don't think so." That door opened and Leanne went in and came back out. "I can't believe she's not home by now. Maybe she and that Louis guy are somewhere out there doing the deed right now."

"I thought you said she was a prude."

"She is, I think. It's hard to tell with her. But she didn't sound that interested in him."

"Maybe he's interested in her. Maybe he made her an offer she couldn't refuse."

Dee heard them kissing and breathing fast. "Something like this," Sandy said.

"Watch it," Leanne said. "She could walk in any minute." Then she laughed real low. "My God," she said, "you're ready to go again?"

"The captain's always ready," Sandy said. His voice was hoarse.

"You tell captain he'll have to wait. Just let me get my medicine and we'll go back to your place and take care of him, all right?"

There was more silence and then a drawer slid open. "I can't believe I forgot it," Leanne said. "Dee and I were talking about her and Louis as I packed up." Leanne was moving things around. "I tried to get her to take one of these."

"Did she?"

"I don't think so. She may be regretting that right about now though." There was the sound of pills shaking in a plastic vial. "Here they are." Leanne was finishing up a round of antibiotics for a strep throat she'd had the weekend before.

"Damn, look at this, Leanne."

"What is it?"

"Her diary. What college girl keeps a diary? It's wide open."

Dee hardly heard anything clearly after that. Her legs felt weak. She thought she heard Leanne say not to read it and then Sandy laughing and reading anyway and Leanne laughing, too, even as she said not to do it. Dee felt trapped in the closet by her own weight and shape.

Leanne and Sandy were arguing now. Sandy read outloud something Dee had written weeks ago, about Sandy being good-looking and Leanne being a lucky girl. Leanne kept asking him to put the diary away and he was saying things about Dee and how he wanted Leanne to act prudish like Dee would and try to stop him and his captain and then Dee could hear they were on the bed. Sandy was calling Leanne Dee and Dee was saying, "No, Louis," and "Don't touch me there, Louis," and they both said cruder things, too, and then the bedsprings and their voices and the wrong names took over the whole room and Dee shrank away in the closet, as thin as one of the dresses hanging next to her.

Dee waited a long time after they were finally gone before she stepped out into the room. They had left all the lights on, and she looked around, feeling she hadn't seen the room before, as if it were a kind of museum with each exhibit demonstrating one of her flaws and defects. Her diary was open on the desk, but not to the current page. Her bedspread was rumpled and both pillows were in the center of the bed. The closet doors stood open.

In the mirror she looked old to herself. For the first time, she saw her mother's face in her own. She had never been able to stare her mother down.

The light at daybreak Saturday was the weakest shade of white, as if the sky was thick gauze and the world was pressed beneath it like a wound. Dee remembered the last things before she fell asleep, the museum feeling and her mother in the mirror. Leanne slept soundly across the room. When she had come back in at six a.m., Dee was still awake but pretended not to be, and Leanne crawled under the covers with her clothes on and fell asleep in seconds. Now Dee stood and pulled the curtains and opened the window as far as it would go. It was snowing lightly and a few snowflakes drifted into the room like confetti after a parade has passed, but Leanne didn't stir. Dee slipped into her cheerleading skirt and sweater and leaned out the window into the snow.

There was no one in sight except for a thin young man who walked across the grass lot between the Fine Arts building and the dorm. He had his hands in his pockets and moved slowly, as if he had been walking all night. Dee saw everything that could happen next—how she could climb out the window and stand up, her bare feet stinging on the cold concrete ledge, how she could pretend she was in the field house at the beginning of her most complicated cheer, slowly leaning into a backward cartwheel. Even if the aimless young man down below looked up and saw her, he wouldn't be able to tell when the leaning became the falling.

Dee slid the window shut and pulled the curtains. She looked in the mirror again. Her mother's eyes were gone now, and what she saw was a young woman in school colors who knew how to forget and how to cheer and how to go right on doing both. She climbed back into bed and pulled the covers around her chin. She closed her eyes and slowed the rhythm of her breathing until it matched Leanne's, breath for breath.

In a few weeks or months, Leanne would remember

nothing about this weekend, not the die-in or the diary
or her drunken time with Sandy in Dee's bed, and Dee
believed the same kind of forgetting was possible for her, too.
She unclenched her fists from the blankets—no one slept
with clenched fists. She tried to picture Leanne's hands,
loose and relaxed, and arrange her own to match. To anyone
looking in or down on them that very moment, Dee was sure
it would be impossible to tell who was the real cheerleader
and who the pretend, or which one slept with Louis and
which with Sandy, or who had cowered in the closet. No
way to tell which woman had imagined the cartwheel out
the window, or who was the junior and who the sophomore.
As long as Dee kept her eyes closed and her fingers half-
curled and each breath measured and controlled, no one in
the world would be able to say which woman was awake and
which woman was asleep.

BETTER FRIENDS

NINE TEN AGAIN

I saw Denny Smith today for the first time in at least a year. He never did grow any bigger.

Who could figure I'd run into Denny today? Just yesterday I signed my enlistment papers, and this afternoon I'm walking through McCormick Park at the center of the old neighborhood and stumble into him. He sat on a bench in front of the ice skating shed. He was watching snowflakes drift onto the frozen lagoon and feeding a flock of park pigeons. They fly all around the big cottonwoods that grow up and down the Clark Fork River. They seem different from the downtown pigeons.

I never have known the hand language Denny uses, but I sat down with him and watched the snow fall for a few minutes anyway. I felt chilly in my parka, although it was warm enough that I could see water filming up on the lagoon ice. Denny didn't seem cold in just a jean jacket. A breeze rattled the last few brittle leaves on the oak trees behind us. For a second I caught a hint of that dusty smell of fall in the park.

A couple of the fattest pigeons came right up and pecked at Denny's canvas shoes. They were the same kind of slip-on deck shoes he had worn that day more than five years ago, but it must have been a different pair. Staring at his shoes though, I kept thinking back to that weekend during the Gulf War when I was in ninth grade, right before or after Easter, I forget which. My buddies and I staged a mock-up war down by the recreation shack in the park. And I lost all my friends.

Denny offered me some stale popcorn to feed the pigeons today, but I said no thanks. I said I had to go, which wasn't really the whole truth.

If I ever said the whole truth, I'd have to say I always used to feel sorry for Denny. It's the kind of sorry with a guilty twist in it that makes you turn your eyes away, even when you know you'll wish you hadn't later. But today, I don't know what I felt. It wasn't sorry. Or guilty. It was something different from both of those.

Who could figure I would ever join the Army? Before this month I'd have probably laughed if anyone even said it. It always seemed like something for other guys—even with all the commercials full of high-tech machines that I do like to watch. But two weeks ago, on a Saturday night at two a.m., when I finished my shift delivering Stagecoach pizzas and didn't have anywhere to go, I walked around all night long. From way out at the Speedway bridge over the river in East Missoula all the way back up to campus. Near dawn I walked by the dorms on Arthur, staring up at the windows, imagining the students asleep in their rooms, and then I headed on out to the very middle of the soccer field on South Street, watching the sun come up. It was trying to snow.

Missoula came clear to me that night. It's the place I've always been. It's the place I have to go away from.

I slept all that Sunday. The next morning I wandered into Southgate mall before most of the stores were even open. The poster at the Army recruiting office hit me in the face like it was waiting for me. The guy in the picture didn't have a doubt in the world. He might have had cares, or even troubles, but he didn't have any doubts. I went inside and talked to them for an hour.

Yesterday was the first day of my nineteenth year. I drove

NINE TEN AGAIN

back over to the recruiters and I signed on the line. It's official now. I take a physical next week, and if everything checks out, in thirty days I get on a Greyhound bus headed for Fort Riley, Kansas. They even pay for the ticket.

~

I tried a semester at the U. here in town. I gave it what my dad calls "a good go," but I didn't have a clue what to even think about for a major, and a 2.0 GPA was the best I could pull. I'm already over a thousand in debt, and it took twenty hours of work a week, delivering pizza for *Stagecoach*, to keep it that low. So maybe Mr. Alston, my advisor over at Hellgate High with the ear warts, wasn't that far off after all. Not everybody is college material.

I carried eighteen credits of mostly Gen-Ed and freshman requirements, and I can't remember one test I wasn't tired for, or turning in a single paper I was proud of. Worse yet, I didn't make a single new friend I could count on. With luck now though, I'll make some real friends, overseas or wherever. In the service you make better friends than anywhere else. My dad says that, and my uncle, and other people do, too. Plus, the Army promises to pay off my school loans. They'll train me in computer science and pay for college later when I want it.

Dad served four years in the Navy in the mid-seventies. Mostly on an aircraft carrier. I don't much like the thought of being on a boat for months though. Still, he read the papers before I signed, and he said it sounded like a pretty good deal. He didn't have much else to say about it, but then, he never does.

I've been working full time at *Stagecoach* and living in my old basement room at the folks' house for two months now. The three of us get along as well as you could expect, but it's not like I can stay forever.

As I stood up from the park bench in McCormick this

afternoon, I told Denny that I had joined the Army and was leaving town. He can hear all right. He handed me a big frosted leaf he was twirling by the stem. I couldn't figure where he'd even found it with all the snow. Then he said something back with his hands. I don't know what. Good luck, I hope.

That's what I said when I left him. Good luck, Denny, I said.

Crossing Hickory Street at the edge of the park, I looked back across the lagoon. I waved and he waved back. From Hickory Street, Denny looked like a little old man.

When I saw him today, I flashed in on something that I couldn't get out of my head during that winter five years ago. I always did that when I was a kid, and maybe I still do. Picking out one thing that doesn't make sense by itself and thinking on it.

I had heard it on the news the weekend or so after our troops finally went in on the ground in Iraq. Some G.I.'s found abandoned bunkers right out in the middle of the desert. Whole bunkers full of carrier pigeons. The only thing they could figure was that the other side was using them to communicate. I remember so clearly lying in my bed that night, imagining the skies over there. First the satellites way up in orbit, snapping pictures and radioing them back. Below that the intelligence planes with their computers and infra-red cameras. Then B-52s and F-111s and all the rest sailing by. Day and night the skies crowded with machines and eyes.

And way down below, just above ground level, those plain pigeons, carrying little messages back and forth.

NINE TEN AGAIN

Denny's a mute as far as I know. Maybe a dwarf, too, but I'm not sure what the cutoff is for that, and it's not the right word to use anymore anyway. He's just real small—under five feet—and he's about my same age, I'm pretty sure.

As far back as I can recall he was always hanging out on the edge of the neighborhood. He went to my grade school, Franklin. The other kids said he had problems besides not being able to talk and being too little. Thinking problems. They sent him to a special school after sixth grade. I never really knew why.

His mother's mute, too. But even if you didn't know that, you could tell they're mother and son. They have the same shaggy sandy hair and dark eyes that don't blink much, like they don't quite see things most people do. Either that or they're seeing things other people don't. They always lived in The Georgia Apartments on Garfield Street. It's a weather-streaked stone building with two half-round towers at the front. It looks like a dirty broken-down castle. She works at a small factory on Ronan Street by the railroad tracks that aren't used anymore. The factory makes little wooden plaques from pieces of scrap wood. They carve kitchen slogans and fishing rhymes in them. Denny works there now too, I heard.

When I sat on the bench with him today and started remembering back, I wondered for just a second if the reason he's stayed so small had anything to do with that one weekend in the park five years ago. But that couldn't be true. His mother isn't much taller than he is.

❦

My friends and I had wanted to play war the whole week. At least a couple of nights after school we met in McCormick on our bikes and talked it up.

That Saturday morning we made battle plans. We pretended the enemy was hiding out in the park, waiting to make a move. There must have been eight or ten of us, but the only names I remember are the Blankenship twins, Tim and Steve. And Mike Thomas.

Those three were the most gung-ho. They rounded up an arsenal for our attack on the rec shack. Tim carried his BB gun under his coat. Steve brought smoke bombs and rolls of ladyfingers he hadn't used on the last Fourth. Mike volunteered some cherry bombs he'd been saving up for the next. The rest of us stockpiled rocks and broken bricks. I brought a baseball bat and a grocery bag full of water balloons I'd filled up at home.

The shack was closed down, of course. In the summer the Parks and Recreation Department checked out equipment for all the games from there. Extra bats and gloves, a tether ball, horseshoes, box-hockey sticks, the four-square ball. In the summer the shack was the center of some of my best times, but in the fall and winter it only reminded me of how far away summer seemed. Like a dream I made up to pass the long afternoons at school.

I can close my eyes right now and see that little square green shack at the base of Wildman's hill by the railroad embankment. We called it Wildman's because of a bike course we built all along it with steep jumps and crazy switch-back turns.

That morning the shack seemed perfect. Steve and Tim declared it Saddam's command and control. We had secret intelligence from our own private spy satellite. The shack was their secret hideout.

We waited by the swings until the courthouse clock across the river struck twelve. We counted down with the chimes. It was noon. Zero hour.

~

First we bombarded the shack from up on Wildman's, creeping down closer and closer. Tim fired BB's as fast as he could. Stones clattered on the shack's roof. Dirt clods ricocheted off its sides. The idea was to make as much noise as possible. Like that Nintendo game Rage Raiders we were all playing. Or all the old war movies about Vietnam.

We split into teams. The Blankenships led the American team, naturally. They were a year older, freshmen at Sentinel High already. Mike Thomas wanted to be a British commander because he'd found a plastic straw that he stuck in his mouth like a cigarette holder. He said things like, "Bloody good show," and "I say, I say."

They made me part of the two-man French team. I couldn't think of anything to do or say to act French except Bon Voyage. I yelled it like a battle cry. "Bon voyage." I threw balloons at the shack. My missiles were locked on targets.

We rode our bicycles by the shack in quick passes, lobbing half-bricks at it. Steve ran up and pushed a lit roll of ladyfingers under the shack, and Tim and I lit a cherry bomb and tossed it on the roof. I remember expecting that someone would show up and scatter us any minute. A patrol car, a park maintenance truck, somebody. But nobody did.

There was a small window with all the glass broken out on the side of the shack opposite the padlocked door. We made a last pass by the shack and sailed a smoke bomb in the window. Steve set a crumpled up Burger King bag on fire and rolled it under one side of the shack. We backed off over by the swings, ready to book. We stood tough and tall, straddling our bikes, laughing and watching our work.

When I first saw the smoke, I figured it was just from Mike's smoke bomb. I didn't know the shack was on fire yet. I'm sure of that. It was right between those two things though, right between seeing the first smoke and hearing Steve laugh about the flames racing up the paint on the shack door, that I saw Denny Smith's face in the window.

He was coughing and trying to climb out the window. He was waving a pair of white underwear like a flag.

❦

Who could figure Denny would be in the Rec shack all by himself? Tim said the little yoyo was probably playing with himself. Mike said he must have hid out from his crazy mother.

I couldn't see why he hadn't tried to get out sooner. Why would a kid sit inside that shack all the time we were terrorizing it and not show his face? He had to have been frightened with all that noise. The walls and roof must have been shaking.

What I finally decided was that he didn't know what was happening. He had no idea. He never ran with the rest of us. We never asked him to play our games. He might just as easy have been thinking it was the end of the world, as figuring out it was only neighborhood guys.

I never asked him if it's true. I've never been able to ask him. But it makes sense to me. If you didn't have any idea what was happening, and you were all alone, then you could imagine almost anything.

❦

Denny kept falling back inside. He must have crawled in through the window all right, but he couldn't seem to get back out. He dropped his underwear out the window. Flames cracked and popped in the air above the door on the other side of the shack.

We just stood there staring, frozen, the way kids will when something they've caused turns into something they never imagined.

Tim said we should get the hell out of there.

Mike said, "What about Denny?"

Tim stood up on his pedals. "What about him?" he said. It seemed like the cruelest thing I'd ever heard anybody say.

I pedalled over to the shack. The air was smoky and hot. I propped my bike up below the window and stood on the pedals and grabbed Denny under the arms. He squirmed on the ledge the way the chubby kids do when they try to pull up out of the swimming pool and can't quite make it. His eyes were full of water and he was shaking. When I dragged him all the way out the window, he didn't have any pants on. I heard one of the guys whistle. They had waited to make sure he was okay after all, but now they scattered for home on their bikes.

It was just Denny and me then. I put him on my handlebars.

He had blue-gray powder marks on his arms. He kept making signs with the fingers of one hand, the same thing over and over. I started off the best I could, but the bike wobbled like I was learning to ride. I didn't know where to go except away from the fire. I heard a siren. Denny must have heard it, too. He kept looking up at the sky.

At the edge of the park I came right up on the fire engine. It was bearing down on us, and I remember wishing Denny had his pants on.

Two firemen hopped down and grabbed Denny and me and put us on the truck. They left my bike on the side of the drive and radioed in for an ambulance. They said Denny wasn't hurt bad. The last I saw of him, they wrapped him in a thick brown blanket and put him up front in the ambulance. They drove off without a siren. I waved to him as they left and he waved back.

A patrol car pulled up. The firemen doused the shack fire in about two minutes flat. There were two big burned spots on one side and a black streak smeared across the roof. Mostly just the paint had burned and blistered.

The firemen rolled up their hose and talked to the policemen. I stood off by myself, leaning up against a big maple tree on the edge of the softball field. I made my mind up. I wasn't going to volunteer anything, but I wasn't going to run either. If they asked, I would tell them.

They took me down to the police station and called my folks to come for me. I gave the names of the other guys. I said I was one of the ringleaders, too. Everybody else's parents received a call, too, but nobody else had to come down. The police visited the other guys' houses later in the week. They explained how vandalism always begins small and how the best time to stop it is before it begins. At least that's what my folks said their folks said.

~

I avoided the Blankenships for over a year after that. They told everybody they were going to beat the hell out of me when they got the chance, and I believed them. Mike Thomas wouldn't speak to me at school for the rest of the eighth grade. I didn't hang out with any of them at the park again, not that spring or the next summer.

Most of those guys went to Sentinel High anyway, that year or the next. I didn't miss them when I started at Hellgate. I found myself at the edge of a whole new crowd there. One that I thought I could be a part of.

Not counting today, I probably only saw Denny half a dozen times since then. Usually when I went by The Georgia Apartments on my bike. Or later in my first car, an old beat-up Datsun pickup. Denny used to sit out on the steps of The Georgia on sunny days.

The last time I saw him before today was one night last winter in my senior year. I ran into him at a bowling alley of all places, the old Westside Lanes on Wyoming Street. It was on a Friday night, and I was on a date with my girlfriend Martha. She went to the university last fall, too, with me, except she's back there again this semester. We broke up just before this Christmas, but still I had been hoping she might give me a call on my birthday. I don't know whether or not I would have told her that I'm leaving for Kansas. I remember her saying one time that the Army was for guys who didn't have anything else going on for themselves.

Denny and his mom were at the alley the time I was with Martha. They were bowling and laughing. They shared popcorn from a brown bag that looked like they had brought it from home. I didn't exactly avoid him, but I was worrying he might come over to our lane or something.

But he didn't. We just waved to each other, like always.

***

I never once told my folks the part about Denny in the shack and me helping him. I think they figured he had been in on it with the rest of us, and I didn't try to explain it any different. Whenever it came up, my dad told me I had done the right thing to tell the names, but his voice never sounded sure about it. Both he and my mother acted like the whole day was just as well forgotten. And I can see that. I know that's true of a lot of days.

Like today on the bench with Denny. Once I leave Missoula and get to Basic Training in Kansas, I won't think of it again. But right now I keep seeing him sitting next to me with the popcorn, and all the park pigeons cooing and pecking around him. He was being friendly, like he remembered, like he was still grateful after all this time.

I think he was trying to make friends with me. He gave me that leaf he liked, and he offered me the popcorn, too. It was quiet there in the park next to him today, with nothing but the new snow and the last leaves. I could have taken the popcorn and fed the pigeons with him.

I should have stayed a little longer. It was the best chance I've had to learn a few of his hand signs. I could have been understood, there on the bench by the pigeons, without even having to speak. Even if it was only with Denny. Even if it was only for one afternoon.

DOGS AND DOGS

NINE TEN AGAIN

Shaded gray light on the dusty concrete underside of the Madison Street bridge. The splash and lap of the river, rushing with spring melt and the tide of night rain. Jen's wet fur, damp and musty-smelling from the early mist. Apple.

Matt cracked his eyes open and squinted beyond Jen at the blossoms on an old half-wild apple tree near the riverbank. On the best mornings, it was like waking up on the first day of a family camping trip, even in the rain. On the worst mornings, it was like waking up on the same camping trip to find your family packed and gone.

Monday morning traffic rumbled over the bridge. Matt pulled his socks on and knelt while he rolled his faded flannel sleeping bag. He found Jen's torn sack of food and tossed two handfuls on the ground, like a farmer scattering chicken feed. While she ate, licking the dusty ground in the rain shadow of the bridge, Matt squatted by the river and rinsed his face and arms and hands, the water cold everywhere but on the tattoos on his forearms, identical profiles of blue eagles. When he stood up again, he felt the nagging pain in his left leg, familiar as a kid brother.

Across the river he saw a Meadowgold dairy truck moving along Front Street. Matt had worked at Meadowgold during his week of on-call day labor two weeks back—loading trucks at the meatpackers for two days and then cleaning the parking lot at the milk plant for three more. His leg had bothered him bad toward that Friday, and the dairy dock foreman caught him sitting down with his boot off more than once. He sent him back to the Job Service office. They said they might have ranch work in the Bitterroot valley soon.

Jen trotted west from the bridge and Matt followed. In the opposite direction on the riverside path, two women in sweatsuits and walkmans ran side-by-side in an easy rhythm. Matt and Jen roamed from McCormick Park to Jacobs Island every day, bumming along the Clark Fork River, sometimes looping through Missoula's small downtown. On an ordinary day, he bought microwave sandwiches and rolling tobacco at Super America on Fourth. On a lucky day, a six-pack of beer, dog food, and a few Lotto tickets at the Food Farm on Fifth.

Behind the locked-up ice skating shed at the kids' lagoon in McCormick, Jen circled a dumpster and Matt retrieved half a burger from a sack near the top of the trash. A man about Matt's age sauntered across the parking lot. Matt followed the man's gaze upward and saw two ducks, beating through the low gray sky, their wingtips inches apart.

This guy looked good for a bill or two. His coat was old, but suede. He wore soft leather gloves and low rubber boots made for walking through water. The ducks disappeared behind a row of tall half-rotten cottonwoods. It looked like it could rain again.

"Say man, how you doing?" Matt shifted his pack and came to a stop with his weight on his good leg.

"Fine enough. It's a beautiful April morning. And yourself?"

"Straight ahead and flat out." Matt set his smile to something near a grimace, an expression he believed would match his slogan. "Say man, could I trade you for some change? Jen and me need a meal—post-pronto." He laughed, motioning to the dog, the burger wrapper between her paws like treasure.

The man reached in his pocket and pulled out the first bill he touched in his wallet, a single. He looked at the dog and pulled out a second one. Matt pocketed the money. They shook hands and introduced themselves.

"Roman like the empire?" Matt asked.

"My grandfather's name," Roman said.

"Well, Roman, I've been hanging under the bridge too long," Matt said, as if they had already been in the middle of a conversation before the money changed hands. "I had a day job week before last, but since then, nada. And then my gear gets ripped." Matt shocked himself sometimes when he heard the lies he told people who gave him money. Yet he liked the feeling, too. It couldn't be that different from what a painter or songwriter must feel when they made up something brand new. "Lucky I had this old pack stashed. I felt it coming, one of those omen deals. I could trade you a blanket."

"No, no. I have a blanket. I have several blankets. You get yourself something to eat."

"It's a drag being broke, you know? I'm thinking of heading out of town—this Misery-oula looks boarded-up to me." Matt waited for Roman's smile. "So far I've been in forty states. You ever been to Alaska?"

Roman nodded. Matt turned and gazed off to the north as if he could see that far.

"That's where I'm headed. They still have the room for opportunity up there. Get on the right crew, I hear a man can really sock it away quick. This crap's old." He waved his arm at everything, the concrete, river, sky. Himself.

"The dog travels with you?"

"More than half a year now. Company. People think living on the street's scary or fast, but when you carve it down, it's just lonesome. You know?" Matt faked a laugh. He had said more than he meant to.

"Sure, I know."

Matt guessed Roman didn't know. He was just killing

time the way people did. Matt liked men well enough but he didn't make friends with them. It took too long. With the right woman, you could get close quick—a kiss or three, a night or two. But men always had to find ways of making out who was winner and loser first, before they found the room for friendship. Yet Matt had plenty of time to kill, too. He kept talking.

"Like the other week when I shacked up, see. I met this honey in Super America, renting movies and charging a six-pack on a Friday night, and I think to myself, this one could write the book on all-by-yourself. But there was no place for the dog, man. No dogs allowed in her apartment house. A guy down the hall shot her with a pellet gun just for barking. Look."

Matt pointed out the scab on Jen's muzzle. "She's OK, but hell, I don't know whether it's worth getting laid if my dog gets shot."

Roman laughed like it was just a story with a good punchline.

"She's healing," Matt said, "but the dog was shot, see for yourself."

"No, I believe you. I can see it." Roman stooped and patted Jen. He rubbed her neck. "She's a retriever, isn't she? Pure?"

Matt stared at Roman's gloved hands. "I don't know for sure. She's a good dog, though."

"Retrievers are good dogs. She'd make an excellent hunter."

"She sniffs the dumpsters like a pro," Matt said. He laughed.

The man stood up, his eyes still on Jen. "That dog deserves better than running alleys and dodging cars," he said. "She may have a bloodline." He drew the word out slowly as if Matt might not understand it. "See how she breathes steady through her nose? That's telltale."

Matt studied Jen. She looked like a stranger's dog. "I

didn't know about that."

"And her eyes are smaller than most," Roman said. "That's another sign. You said you wanted to trade me something." He pointed at Jen.

Matt stepped back and Jen did, too. "For two bucks? Not this year. Do you practice up on that sense of humor, or does it just roll out natural for you? "

Roman made as if to laugh again, but his eyes didn't follow through. "It sounds like I've insulted you," he said. "But I didn't mean for two dollars." He reached for his wallet again and held it in his hand. "I'd give you more."

This time Matt didn't want to look. Wallets and purses, everywhere you looked they were opening and closing. Little leather mouths that did the real talking in the world.

"Just because I'm busted don't mean my dog's for sale, pal."

"I was just offering." Roman turned away. "But you know friend, there's dogs and then there's dogs." He waved his arm toward the houses above the park. "Missoula's thick with them. The paper has free ones every morning. And the shelter gives them away right and left." He pointed west, downriver, the direction the ducks had flown.

"So how much more are we talking about?"

Roman brushed his gloved fingers around Jen's mouth, exposing her gums from one side to the other. He raised her pads and looked at them. Matt didn't like the way he touched her.

"Twenty dollars more?"

"Forget it. We're not a walking yard sale here." Matt flashed a glinty look and swallowed hard, a metallic, baking-soda taste way back in his throat. He sized Roman up, the placement of his feet, the bend of his knees. He gauged his reach and inched back till he was just beyond it.

Roman kept his eyes on Jen. "Okay." He looked back in his wallet. "I'll give you forty-eight dollars, fifty total, a good deal all around. I could use a retriever come fall. And she'd be a good dog with my daughter."

Matt thought of his day wages—about forty dollars take-home. Fifty meant more than a full eight hours on his feet. He considered palming the money and splitting with Jen. But no, this Roman lived around here. He'd fetch the cops. One thing Matt prided himself on was staying clear of jail. He extended his hand, and Roman shook it again without taking off his glove.

"Thanks for both the Georges," Matt said. "But Jen's not for sale. Retriever or no."

Roman dropped his hand. "I guess there's no helping some people out," he said, stepping away, shaking his head. "Even with the best intentions."

They stood a few feet apart now—outside the circle Matt had imagined—there would be no fight. But Matt didn't want to let him have the last word either.

"Yeah, and there's a golden ladder leads right up out of hell, too," he said. He wasn't sure what it meant, but he'd known a bartender in Tulsa who always said it at exactly the right moment. It was the kind of idea that could mean lots of different things, and people didn't usually have a comeback for it.

Roman took another step away. He pointed at the dog, circling Matt's feet. "She's likely past teaching anyway."

Matt matched him with another step back. He tensed his leg to cover his limp. A guy like this you needed to keep up with or he'd find a way to take advantage.

"The best ones are," he said. "That's what you guys never know."

Roman waved his hand as if he could push Matt away from a distance.

"C'mon, Jen," Matt said, turning away, smiling as the dog fell in behind him, feeling as good about the forty-eight bucks he had refused as the two he'd taken. If you didn't take the little victories to heart, you'd never know a big one when it came your way. He waited. Roman didn't say anything else. One more for good measure. Matt yelled over his shoulder.

"See you at the hunt, man."

∼

By noon the sky cleared and the sun stood straight overhead like a yellow hole at the top of a big blue tent. The day was gathering heat for a run at the afternoon. Coming out of Super America, Matt stopped to small talk with a man gassing up a motorhome. A teenage boy watched from the passenger seat. The leather cover on the spare tire read *The Getaway*.

Before Matt finished his pitch, tires squealed on Fourth Street. Matt looked up just as a blue Tempo knocked Jen to the curb. He dropped his pack by the pumps and ran to her. She lay nestled in next to the curb, breathing heavy like she'd run a long way without water. There was no blood, but her eyes flickered from side to side without blinking.

"Easy, baby, easy." Matt lifted her two front legs slowly, one at a time. They didn't feel busted. A woman in fine summery clothes stepped out of the blue car. Matt saw a flash of thigh as quick as a promise, but he didn't enjoy it the way he usually would. She hurried over to them.

"God, I'm so sorry. He ran in front of me. Is he all right?"

"She's a she. I don't know. She don't look good."

The woman reached her hand out. Jen growled.

"Leave her be," said Matt. "We'll be OK. She may need some food though. You wouldn't have an extra few, would you?"

The woman hesitated, shivering in light clothes. "My purse is in the car." She pointed over her shoulder. "Her breathing's rough. I'm worried about your dog."

"So am I."

The woman went toward her car. The *Getaway* man

came out with Matt's pack at arm's length and set it down. He had a silver credit card between his fingers.

"I'll call the Humane Society. We've got a phone in the rig."

"No — don't do that."

"The dog needs help. It took a good shot." The man's trimmed salt-and-pepper hair ran flat and straight, close to his head. Even the creases in his slacks looked first-class. Matt felt messed-up. His life was junk in a world where all the rest was combed out smooth.

The trim man went back toward the pumps. Matt didn't say anything else. As he watched the woman hurry back over with three dollar bills clutched in her hand, he saw Roman standing across the street, staring from the doorway to a used book store.

"I'm short of cash," she said. "Should I call somebody?"

"What?" Matt looked up at the woman. He folded the bills with one hand and put them in his shirt pocket. He kept the other hand steady on Jen, stroking her head. "No need. Thanks."

"Listen, I'm late for an appointment. Should I stop back afterward?"

"We'll be gone by then." Matt looked across the street, but he didn't see Roman again.

~

They wouldn't let Matt ride in the Humane Society van — insurance regulations, the driver said. The attendant said the dog would survive — the bumper had just tagged her on the shoulder and shaken her up good. They gave Matt the Animal Shelter phone number and address. It was four miles away. Matt sat on the curb, chewing a strip of beef jerky he had saved out for Jen.

On the way back down to the river, he stopped at the Job Service, a low brick building in an old residential neighborhood on Third Street. The man at the counter had sweat circles under the arms of his dress shirt. He told Matt they were still waiting on the call for ranch hands in the valley. He couldn't talk because he had to give a typing test in a few minutes.

After sundown Matt built a small close fire in a low hidden spot among poplar trees and willow brush near the waterline. In the flickering light he stared at the eagles on his arm as if they might take off at any moment and listened to the river rush by like it had a certain place to go to. He tried not to worry about Jen. Instead he went over the only two other important things he could think of, his plan and his past.

The plan he could put in a single word. Alaska. He had been headed that way for two months, following the spring north and west from a tough, achy winter on a tree-planting crew in Alabama. In a month he would turn forty, and he had made it up in his mind to be in Alaska on that birthday. As for the past, he was still hoping to get that back. He had lost his first thirty-five years, or all memory of them, which amounted to the same thing as far as Matt could tell. In the spring of '97, he had appeared to himself in a St. Louis hospital mirror, a damaged man with eagle tattoos, a limp in his left leg, and a fresh white bandage wrapped around his head like a turban.

He had been found in the I-70 median with nothing but his clothes and one letter in his pocket—a Charlie Brown birthday card that said "Happy 35th to Matt—Love, Jenny." Matt took his name from that card and his birthday from the day they said found him, May 11.

The police traced his fingerprints, but all anybody could tell him was that he didn't have a police record and he had never been in the Service. Matt had hoped he was a veteran when he saw the tattoos. He thought he might have some government money coming, or maybe be some kind of hero who had lost his medals, along with his memories.

Jen had stumbled onto him while he slept under a roadside picnic bench outside of Guymon in the Oklahoma panhandle the summer before, and he named her for the mystery woman who gave him a name and an age. There had been enough real women since the birthday card though, starting with Liz Shelden, a barmaid he met the week he was discharged from the hospital. Thirty-five years old, and he couldn't know whether he was a virgin or not, although Liz seemed to think not.

Matt believed his limp brought out the mother in women, and too, they always seemed to want to help him find out about the lost years. The woman he spent the longest time with, JJ Duncan, had promised him it would all come to him one night in her bed, right at the supreme moment of pleasure, she said. He stayed with her for over a year in Trinidad, Colorado, believing she might be right. She waited counters at a truck stop, but she said she had some gypsy in her, and Matt believed her about that, too. She told Matt she saw flashes about his life when they made love— she was sure it was pretty close to the surface. When she got near to her own moment, she would press her palms on either side of Matt's head, as if she could coax all those lost years out into her fingers, like an old-time poultice pulling on a wound.

It turned out when Matt came to know her well enough that she had an awful lot she needed to forget. Her old man had screwed her once every year on her birthday from when she was five until she ran away at fifteen. He told her that if she breathed a word to anyone he would stash her in an orphanage and no one would ever come see her. One night when Matt came in from his job on a sheep ranch outside Trinidad, he found JJ kneeling in a slump over the toilet. Red fingerprints smeared the flush handle, and a bloody wire cheese knife lay on the tile next to her. When Matt pulled JJ's head up, her face was as white as mashed potatoes and her forearms disappeared into the scarlet water of the toilet bowl. Matt laid her down on the bathroom floor and folded her arms against her chest. He had covered her with two big towels and kissed her cold forehead before he packed and left.

Sometimes Matt thought he was actually the lucky one. A lot of the people he had known in the last five years were spending half their time trying to forget something. And it seemed just as hard for them to forget as it was for Matt to remember.

Matt walked along South Third Street toward the Animal Shelter. For three days straight, he had called from a pay phone to check on Jen, and now he was determined to get her back. They said the dog was all right, but they were concerned she had no record of shots or tags and they wanted to know Matt's address. He told them she'd had her shots in Oklahoma, and he gave them an address from a house near the river on Second Street. The lady on the shelter phone said they would need I.D. or other proof of a local address before they could release the dog.

Two boys on a bike too big for either of them rode toward him on the sidewalk. The larger one pedalled standing up, puffing hard to keep the bike straight, while the smaller one balanced on the handlebars. They looked like brothers, and Matt turned and watched them until they disappeared. The soft-headed feeling children gave him, like the urge he felt to protect Jen, made Matt believe he could have been a father once himself. He sometimes daydreamed about coming across kids of his own by accident. He liked to imagine he would know their names without asking, and that the names would trigger an avalanche of memory inside him, his past falling into place for him all at once, like boulders settling in a creek bed.

As the houses thinned out and the yards grew bigger

along River Road, Matt came up with a plan for getting Jen back. He would say the starter in his car had checked out and he had left his wallet in the glove box. No one would press it all that hard over a dog. The wheeler-dealer Roman had said the place damn near gave them away. Matt just needed to show up in person and make his claim.

He had missed Jen bad that morning when he woke up without her under the bridge, and what had awakened him hadn't made it any better. It was a dream about the time in Denver when Jen had been lost for almost a week, the week the smog had been so bad Matt thought maybe the world was ending, the kind of dark, fearsome weather they talked about somewhere in the Bible. In the dream he didn't find her again, though. Instead he met JJ, wandering the streets, looking for him. Her face and lips glowed pale white. She ran to Matt when she saw him and said she'd remembered his past, that she had it all in her head as real as a movie. Her hands stretched out to him like she was trying to clap. She had Matt's eagle tattoos on the inside of both her wrists.

He heard barking before he even started up the long gravel drive that led to the Animal Shelter. An acre of lawn stretched beneath Chinese elm trees in front of the building. Matt nodded and smiled at a woman in white slacks walking a miniature collie.

Inside the office, it was too hot, and the woman at the counter wouldn't budge on the proof of address. Plus she acted put out because he hadn't come sooner. She told him they had already put the red dog—she wouldn't call her Jen—up for adoption.

"That was a retriever, I believe?"

"One hundred per cent," Matt said. The top button of the woman's blouse was undone. Matt checked her out when she bent over to look up the file.

"In fact," she said, straightening up and looking at him with an index card in her hand. Her fingers drifted to her open button. "In fact," she repeated, "you're too late. A family took her this morning. I just came on shift at noon." Matt had looked away, but now he stared at the card in her hand. "They paid for her shots and license. A man with his daughter. A very nice home."

"Nice or no, that's pretty quick, isn't it? Four days?"

"Quicker than usual, perhaps. But the dog had no license or records." She looked at the card again. "Apparently this was someone who had seen her brought in."

"Seen her? Who would that be?"

"We're not allowed to give out any names." She tapped the card against her fingernail.

"That's cool," Matt said. "That's fine. I was just surprised anybody but me knew she was here." He hesitated for a moment. "You ever had a dog of your own, Miss?"

"Mrs." she said. "Why?"

"I just wondered. Working around so many dogs. You must really love them."

"I'm more of a cat person, actually. We have two at home."

"Two keep each other company."

"That's true." She smiled for the first time. Matt watched her slip the card back into the file. The corner edge stuck up just enough to see.

"Well, thanks anyway, I guess. If she's out to a good home like you said, maybe it's that much better." He started for the door and then turned back. "Oh yeah, did you all keep my collar she was wearing?"

"She didn't have any tags," the woman said. "What collar?"

"It was braided leather. Just a plain braided collar, black and dark brown. But it was almost new. I'd like to have it back if it's still around here."

"I don't know," she said. "I'll check."

She opened a door and disappeared down a long aisle between cages. Before she shut the door, the animal smells wafted into the office as thick as if they'd been bottled. Matt leaned over the counter and pulled out the index card on Jen. He read the name and address on the card: Roman Cleed, 223 Rollins. He shook his head as he slid the card back into the file box.

"Sneaky son of a bastard," he said under his breath. He moved away from the counter, but the woman still didn't return. Matt paced the length of the room, looking at pictures of pets on the wall, perfect Springer Spaniels on point and petite Siamese cats with mysterious eyes. A large glass donation jar with a slot cut in the lid stood on the counter, and Matt unscrewed the lid and counted eight ones. He thought of all the animals behind the door. Fifty-fifty felt fair. He pocketed four of the bills and replaced the lid. He stepped away again just as the woman came out from the back rooms.

"No one remembers seeing any kind of collar with the red dog," she said.

"No big deal," Matt said. "Thanks anyway." He walked to the door quickly.

"I don't think there was any collar," the woman said to Matt's back.

"Mr. Bloodline probably stole that, too," he said as he shut the door.

By the time Matt found the house on Rollins, he was short of breath and dragging his leg worse than usual. He limped up three steps and knocked loudly on the door and then pressed the bell twice. When Roman answered, Matt spoke first.

"I'm here for my dog."

"She's not your dog anymore," Roman said. He stepped out on the porch. "You nearly got her killed anyway. It was just a matter of time. And how did you get my address?"

"There's a way to every will, buddy. I don't want any trouble. Just give me back my dog and I'm gone." He pointed into the house.

"First, I'm calling the Humane Society," Roman said. "They need to hear about this. And then if you don't get off my porch right now, I'll call the police, too."

Matt swallowed hard and stared straight in Roman's eyes. "Lots of things can happen between the calling and the coming," he said.

Roman's face went rigid. He looked Matt over as if to see if he might have a knife or a gun. Matt wanted to play it right on the edge, just enough fear to get the dog and go but not enough to get the guy really worked up. He backed up a step and started whistling for Jen.

As Roman turned to latch the storm door, Jen pushed through it and ran out of the house. She barked twice and threaded between Roman's legs and leapt up on Matt. He grabbed her behind the neck and rubbed her roughly, smiling.

"Hey, Jen, yeah, it's me," he said, "it's me."

The door opened again and a little girl stepped onto the porch. She wore a cone-shaped, foil-covered party hat with a thin elastic strap pulled around her chin.

"Who's this, Dad? Is he a friend of Goldie?"

Roman put his hands on his daughter's shoulders and held her. Matt said "Down," in a deep voice, and Jen sat at his side. The four of them looked at each other. The girl's grin looked to Matt as if he had rung her doorbell right between the presents and the candles. He felt the hint of a memory, not a real picture of a birthday party, yet something close.

"I'm an old friend," Matt said. "I've been taking care of her."

"This is my girl, Beth," Roman said. "You caught us at a bad time. We're having a little party. It's her half-birthday this Friday."

Beth laughed. "It's not a bad time," she said. "It's a good time. I have a dog. A dog of my own." She grabbed Jen by the neck and put her arms around her. Matt stepped back to the edge of the steps and watched her.

"Happy birthday," Matt said. "How old and a half are you?"

"Eight and a half," Beth said. She looked up at Matt. "Did you know Dad in the war?" She pointed at her father, but didn't pause for an answer. "Were you in the war in the desert with him?" She pointed up the street, as if the Middle East might start somewhere right in the next block. "Did you hurt your leg there with him?" She pointed at Matt's leg, although he thought he'd been standing straight enough. "Do you know how old Goldie is? My dad says two." Finally, she caught her breath.

Matt laughed out loud. "You got a whole barrel full of questions, don't you?" He stroked Jen's head. "Two sounds about right," Matt said. "You call her Goldie?

"I named her," Beth said. She looked at Jen and then back up to Matt. "Did she have another name?"

"Well, I called her—" Matt stopped. If he didn't tell them her name, it would be like not really giving her up to them. They'd only get themselves a red dog, a retriever. "I called her all sorts of names."

"C'mon, Bethie, let's go in," Roman said. "You don't have a coat on."

She grabbed Jen by her collar and pulled. They both moved toward the door and then inside. Matt and Roman stood motionless, both looking at the dog until she disappeared into the house. Beth turned around at the door.

"Do you want a piece of my half-birthday cake?" she asked.

"No, I'm going," Matt said, "I'm gonna be going. I'm on

my way to Alaska. I just stopped over to meet you and see how she's doing." He pointed in the house after Jen and smiled at Beth. He started down the steps, his pack on one shoulder.

"Bye," Beth yelled. She went into the house, and Roman closed the door behind her. Matt heard Jen bark again.

"Thanks," Roman said. "That was decent of you."

Matt looked up from the bottom step.

"There's people and there's people," he said. He turned away.

Roman shouted after him. "I could give you a lift somewhere." He pointed at his van.

Matt looked at the van, then back at the house. "I'll walk."

"Wait," Roman said. "Hold on just a minute now." He turned and went in the house. Jen came to the storm door and stared out.

Matt could see a little way into the house behind Jen. He couldn't shake the excited look on the girl's face, that birthday look. It almost felt like he remembered someone giving him a dog when he was a kid, but he couldn't tell. It could have been from a dream or maybe just a TV show he he'd seen and forgotten.

Roman came back. This time he stepped carefully through the door so Jen wouldn't get out. He was carrying a piece of chocolate cake on a paper plate.

"She really wants you to have a piece of cake," he said, holding it toward Matt. Roman handed him a napkin, too, and Matt saw a flash of green folded in it. With one hand he thumbed the bills, five tens. As he did, Roman walked quickly back up on the porch and stood beside the door. Beth and Jen were at the storm door again, too.

Matt watched the three of them watch him, all facing the same direction, the way a family would. Beth waved and Matt held up the plate with the cake and nodded toward her. He slipped the bills in his pocket and ate the cake in three big bites and wiped his mouth with the napkin. Roman had gone inside, but the girl and the dog stayed at the door, watching Matt, so he waved again, exaggerating, swinging the plate back and forth as if he was directing traffic or signaling someone far-off. He saw Beth laughing although he couldn't hear her. The plate slipped out of his hand, and he bent to pick it up. When he looked up again, the inside door was closed.

There was no one in sight up and down the block. Matt folded the paper plate up small and stuffed it in his jacket pocket. He didn't look back again until he had turned the corner behind a long row of thick lilac bushes in heavy bloom, and then when he did, he couldn't see the house. The bushes next to him smelled sweet. He wanted to believe he could still hear the girl's laughter, somewhere on the breeze, drifting.

BRIDGESTONE, 1963

NINE TEN AGAIN

In the summer of 1963 some of the gas stations in my hometown of Lincoln, Nebraska, rented motorbikes—50-cc Hondas, or 80s, or 110s—with small noisy engines that sounded like cheap chainsaws. They popped up everywhere at once. My friends from high school rented them. You had to pay ten bucks an hour, show a driver's license, and sign a fine-print liability waiver. The waivers must not have worked though because by the next summer most of the rentals were gone.

My mother wouldn't let me rent the motorbikes. I'd passed the driver's test in May, the Monday after my sixteenth birthday, and my license burned like a badge in my pocket, but the best I could hope for was to drive her Bel-Air with her in it. She didn't trust me not to take it out by myself and die on her, she said, and now I think she may have been only half-joking, though at the time I thought she was simply afraid I might run off with no warning as my father had.

She had said no to the motorbikes even before a nineteen-year-old in Omaha, sixty miles away, died on one in early June, but she made a point to leave the morning paper open on the breakfast table the next day. The boy hit a convertible and wound up in its backseat, his neck broken. The newspaper photo showed his smashed motorbike and a dark-headed teenage girl who had been riding in the backseat of the convertible, her pink sundress smeared with his blood.

At the very end of that June, my mother had a hysterectomy. She was about to turn forty: a good-looking woman, her shoulder-length hair still jet black, and long, trim legs. Showgirl legs, I'd heard my father call them years before.

All she told me was that her doctor hadn't liked some test result or other and had given her only the one option. Right before the Fourth of July she came home from the hospital, a changed woman, although I couldn't see the actual change, of course, and I only saw her scar once. She went back to work within the week, but for the rest of that summer, she refilled two prescriptions: pink-and-black capsules for pain and off-white tablets for mood. She finished the fifth of Old Granddad that had been in the back of the broom closet since the New Year's Eve before my father left, more than five years earlier. She bought more.

A clerk at the city payroll office, my mother had often brought her work home—weekly payroll tapes to run on the adding machine she set up on the kitchen table, verifying them to the penny. That summer she quit bringing the tapes home.

It took me a while to realize I missed it. For years I'd been hearing the click of her fingernails on the keys and the mechanical cough of the machine each time it totaled. I usually helped her roll the tapes back up when she was done, rubberbanding them tightly and handing them to her. I think listening to her work on the tapes reassured me, as if everything could be counted up and put to rest, sooner or later, though I don't think I thought of it that way then.

～

Near midnight on the last day of August, a Thursday, we left for Colorado Springs, driving at night to avoid the heat. My mother had to be back at work on Tuesday, and school started for me the same day. I wasn't sure I wanted to be going. Since my father left, we had spent two short summer vacations together, one in a fancy hotel in Kansas City and one at Spirit Lake in Iowa. This time though, my mother said, we'd see the mountains. I told myself this was the last summer I would vacation with my mother. I wondered if they had motorbikes for rent in Colorado.

Bugs battered the windshield and dried to thin scabs in seconds. Across Nebraska, we alternated driving every few hours, my mother pretending not to watch the speedometer when I drove. At dawn we crossed the Colorado state line, the farthest west I'd ever been. From there I drove all the way to Colorado Springs. By the time we pulled up at the Broadmoor Resort and parked under one of the fringed awnings, my left arm was red from the sun.

"It's bigger than in the picture," my mother said as she pulled out the brochure they had mailed her. The cars in the parking area shone like colored mirrors. The '58 Bel-Air my father had left us with seemed much older than it was.

"Looks expensive," I said.

"Seventy-five dollars," she said, running her finger down the lines in the rate chart. "But we can afford one night of the finest."

I opened the door and stepped onto the asphalt. "We're out of place," I said as I walked in front of the car and started toward the hotel.

"Cane?"

She was waiting for me to be chivalrous. I went to her side of the car and opened her door. She swung her legs out, pulling up the strap on one of heels.

"That's the point," she said, standing and smoothing her skirt.

"What? Opening the car door?"

"To be out of place for once," she said.

I rolled my eyes, something I did often around her then. She took my arm and we walked toward the entrance.

"It's only one day out of our lives," she said. "Pretend you're in a movie."

I spent most of the afternoon in and out of the largest of the Broadmoor's swimming pools, lying in a blue vinyl lounger, drinking Pepsi, and wishing my way through women's bathing suits from behind my sunglasses.

My mother hadn't brought a bathing suit. She only came out to the pool in the evening, wearing a long-sleeved sweater. We sat at a wrought-iron patio table with a pink canvas umbrella.

A tall waiter in a white coat and black bowtie took our order. The cocktails on the drink card were named after mountains. I asked for another Pepsi. My mother ordered a Pike's Peak, a rum mix that was listed on the card as Pike's Peak of Passion. It came in a wide glass filled with crushed ice, a small paper parasol at its side. The waiter set the glass down with a flourish. I couldn't tell if he was flirting with her or making fun of her.

There were two straws in the drink, and my mother offered me a sip. When she left for the bathroom, her heels clicked across the floor like the telegraph sets in old western movies. The waiter looked years younger than my mother, but he watched her from behind. I sipped at her drink while she was gone.

On the way back to our wing of the hotel, we stopped in a courtyard and sat on a metal bench with intricate scrollwork on its back. I was feeling the rum a little—that or the thinner air. I looked around and took it all in: the sky deep with stars, the feathered outlines of the mountains, the well-dressed people strolling the hotel grounds like dolls. Their voices carried, light and airy, on the cool breeze. I couldn't imagine any of them ever being angry or sick. I tipped my head back and gazed straight up at the sky. The world was finer and cleaner than I was used to. I liked it and yet it made me nervous, like being in a shop filled with cut glass.

"My goodness," my mother said, "it's beautiful."

I'd almost forgotten she was next to me. I turned and said the first thing that came to my mind. "You look different," I pointed away from the mountains, "than at home."

"They call it happy," she said, still clutching the little parasol from her drink. "Like something I borrowed. The first time this summer." She twirled the parasol. "Maybe in years."

"Since Dad left?" In Lincoln I wouldn't have said it. We didn't mention my father. I had always followed her lead. If you can't say something good, zip it up.

My mother laughed, but it wasn't real. "Was I happy then?" she asked.

A redheaded girl about my age walked toward us. I recognized her from the pool before. She looked uncomfortable in heels. I watched her without turning my head, and I shifted on the bench, crossing my leg, an ankle on one knee, the other knee pointed at my mother. The girl didn't look our way.

My mother had pulled her medicine out of her purse. She shook two pills into her palm. "I need water," she said. She stood up. "I'm going in now."

I stared at her hand with the pills in it.

"At least I was whole then," she said.

This was the newer thing we didn't speak of. A run of hazy images flipped through my mind, things I could never have seen: a surgeon's blade, the hospital garbage, her empty space. I closed my eyes hard.

She touched my shoulder. "Cane, this trip's for you, too." She sighed, as if having to tell it to me marked some kind of failure on her part. "Tomorrow won't be like this. We can't afford this." She looked around. "I want you to be happy, too. Are you?"

"This hotel could be boring anyway," I said, standing up. "But I like the West. I like driving the car."

"I know you do," she said. We walked toward the nearest door. I opened it and held it for her as she walked through ahead of me.

"I'm not like him," I said from behind her.

We crossed the foyer. The thick carpet swallowed the sound of our footsteps. I pressed the elevator button. A bell chimed somewhere above us.

"I know you're not," she said.

～

I hadn't seen or heard of my father in over five years, and as far as I knew, neither had my mother. The evening he left us, he'd been working in the basement of our duplex, refinishing an ash dining-room table he bought at a moving sale. Some fool had not recognized its value and painted it over, he said. I lay upstairs on the living-room rug.

"I need to go out now," my father said, closing the door to the basement stairs.

"It's a work night," my mother said. She thumbed an issue of *Photoplay* magazine under a narrow cone of light from one of the pole lamps in the corner.

"Steel wool," he said. He leaned over her chair and kissed her cheek. "I need more solvent and wool."

He bent to kiss the top of my head, too. On the TV show I was watching, a man with piercing eyes had hypnotized all the children in a small town. My father smelled of paint stripper, acrid and flammable. At the door he lit an Old Gold cigarette.

"You taking the car?" my mother asked.

A commercial compared toothpaste to a giant glass shield. My father tossed his spent match at an ashtray. It landed between the rug and the wall.

"No," he said, "I need to walk these dogs." He looked at his boots.

Nobody said anything more. If we had been in our own

comic book—the way I most often liked to imagine things when I was eleven—the balloon rising above each of us would have been blank. Or filled with question marks.

I shuffled my knees across the rug and reached out to the doorknob he held. A small yellow spark snapped at my fingertips. My father laughed and winked at me, and then he turned and walked away across the front lawn.

The hypnotic man on TV confessed, as he led all the town's children across a long wooden bridge, that he actually came from a distant planet. The children's eyes became fiercer, too, like his, and they kept following him across the bridge. I fell asleep watching them.

I woke up in my bed, my mother's voice way too loud in the kitchen. "You rat!" she said, "you've lied." I rolled over, waiting for my father's voice. Morning light worked through the closed Venetian blinds. "Please," she said, "please, now." I still didn't hear my father.

Then the phone receiver slammed down, and the kitchen faucets went on full blast. I remember thinking that maybe she was doing the dishes, but the sink wasn't filling. It wasn't water on water. It was all running down the drain.

I padded into the kitchen, acting groggier than I was. "Mom?"

Her back was to me. She turned the water off and reached for a box of Wheaties and filled two bowls without turning around. My father hadn't needed steel wool, she said, hadn't gone to the hardware store, hadn't come home all night. The side of her jaw went slack and tense the way I had only seen my father's go before. Then she turned to me, her eyes bright and wet. My father wouldn't be home, she said. Not for a while anyway, she said.

∽

Late the next morning in Colorado we found the Rock Garden Motel. They charged sixteen dollars a night for a two-bedroom log cabin off by itself. The nearest trees were on the far side of a rocky lot full of empty propane tanks, but my mother liked the rustic little cabins. And the Garden of the Gods natural formations park was only a few miles away. She had a brochure about that, too. She paid in advance for two nights without noticing what I saw the minute we drove up. The Dino station across the highway had a whole row of motorbikes for rent.

She went to the motel office for ice and coat hangers while I nosed around my room. Lines of rust stained the metal stall in the little bathroom between the sleeping rooms. There was no phone or TV. A yellow D-Con ant trap lay upside down in the metal closet. I spread out on the lumpy mattress, listening to traffic.

When I woke up and went to the porch, fat shadows splayed across the gravel in the motel yard. My mother stood on the porch, a drink in her hand.

"What time is it? I asked. "I fell asleep."

"Almost four," she said. "It's the altitude. We're not used to it."

I sat down in a chair made from the same kind of logs as the cabin.

"You'll get splinters," she said, pointing at the other chair. "I already ran my hose." She bent her knee, lifted her calf behind her, and stared down at a jagged line in her stocking. For a moment I thought she looked ridiculous. It was a warm afternoon and she stood on a log-cabin porch in heels and nylons.

When she stepped back inside, I gazed at the station across the highway, mentally counting the twenty-five dollars of my paper-route money folded in my pocket. I followed her into her room.

I looked around for anything different from my room. I saw an exposed water pipe near the ceiling in one corner, a very faint stain on the bedspread. My mother poured another drink and dropped two ice cubes in it.

"You're starting early," I said.

"This place is early," she said. She moved to the dresser. She had laid out her pills. She picked up the white one with her fingernails.

"I want to rent a bike," I said. I pointed at the doorway.

She put the tiny pill on her tongue and washed it down. "A bike?"

"A motorbike," I said. "I have my own money."

"Where're you pointing?" she asked. She sat down on the bed and sank into it, spilling a few drops of her drink on the place where the bedspread was already stained. She moved away from the spot. The bedsprings creaked.

"Right across the highway," I said. "Just for an hour."

"You know the answer," she said.

"I have a license and my own money. What could you do about it?"

"Cane, please drop it. Let's go see the Garden of the Gods. You can drive the car both ways, there and back. They say it's gorgeous. The rocks look like things." In her eyes I thought I saw a little girl. It took me by surprise.

"I'll go if I can rent a bike first," I said. The cabin door was wide open. A rectangle of yellow light lay askew across the gray linoleum floor. "This would be the perfect place to ride."

"So I have to make deals?" she said. "I pay all this money to bring us out here and you're telling me what you'll do for me?"

"I didn't ask to come," I said. My voice sounded cold and flat to my own ear, and I thought then that I wouldn't rent the bike. She wouldn't agree to it, and I wouldn't disobey her.

"It's too dangerous," she said. "Period. I'm not going to sit here in this knotty-pine rattrap and worry about you."

"Just have another drink," I said. "And another pill."

"You're being cruel," she said.

"Honest," I said. It struck me we were both right.

"I want to go see that Garden," she said, "the red rocks." She picked up the brochure she had been looking at earlier and held it out. On the cover was a picture of two rocks shaped something like animal heads leaning into each other. The caption read *The Kissing Camels*.

"Go by yourself," I said. I walked out. I bought a can of Pepsi outside the motel office and sauntered over to the barbecue area. Five log chairs circled a rock fire pit. Where they weren't blackened by fire, the rocks were a shade of rose I'd never seen before. I sat down with my back to the cabin, the Bel-Air, my mother. I stared at the half-burnt logs in the fire pit, remembering a weekend years before with my father at Lewis and Clark Lake on the Nebraska-South Dakota border. I must have been only six or seven, and the first night by the lake, the sound of the waves lapping in the dark frightened me. The more scared I was, the more wood my father put on the fire. A big, hot fire would keep anything away, he said. This is what men had always done, all the way back to the cave days, he'd said.

A pickup pulled into the motel circle and kept going, its tires crunching the red gravel like hard nuts. At the far cabin, a couple with white hair sat on their porch, playing cards on a polished tree-stump table. I looked over my shoulder. My mother's door was closed.

I walked back to our cabin and went into the bathroom and stood over the toilet, listening. I flushed the toilet. Still nothing. I knocked and then walked into her room. She slept on the bed, her clothes on. The other pill was gone from the bureau, and her bottle was half-empty. I stepped back through the bathroom, closing both doors behind me.

~

Fifteen an hour, the attendant said. I told him I would think about it. I walked to the bikes at the far side of the lot and looked at one of the 80-cc's. I had my twenty-five dollars folded in my shirt pocket. I checked the shift levers. I was pretty sure I knew how they worked.

"Gonna rent one?"

A short, bulky man stood behind me. He wore wire-rimmed sunglasses, a white T-shirt, jeans, and pull-on leather work boots. He looked sunburned. He might have been thirty.

"I haven't decided," I said.

"Too pricey?" the man asked, smiling.

"Fifteen an hour," I said.

"D'you see mine?" He pointed at a larger bike at the pumps. It was red and white and had a fat chrome pipe curving away from the engine on each side. A small pack and a rolled sleeping bag were tied to the bike with rawhide laces. The man moved toward it, talking. "It's got more get-up-and-go than all those put together," he said.

I followed him to his bike. He straddled it, turned the key, and kick-started it. The engine made a deep rumbling sound.

"What kind is it?

"Bridgestone. 350 cc. Fine craftsmanship. Only two years old. I bought it from a fool who never rode the damn thing." He laughed. "Not man enough, I guess." He spun the throttle and the engine roared. "I still get a kick showing it off," he said and grinned. "Excuse my manners." He held his hand out toward me. "I'm Jack Garvey out of Dallas, Texas."

I shook his hand. "Cane Roane," I said. "I'm from Nebraska."

"Cane," Jack said. "There's one you don't hear. Like in the Bible?"

"Like the walking stick," I said. "It's my father's name. A name in our family."

"Those are the best," Jack said. "Where you staying?"

I pointed across the highway at the Rock Garden.

"They want too much money for my blood," Jack said. "I checked it out this afternoon." A Ford Fairlane pulled into the pumps behind us. Jack pushed the cycle off its stand and edged it forward. I walked along next to him.

"I just toured that Garden of the Gods place," Jack said.

"That's where my mother wants to go," I said.

"Lord to say, it is something. Those rocks look like anything you could imagine. Where's your mother?"

I pointed across the highway again.

"That pretty lady drinking on the porch this afternoon?" Jack pointed, too. "I spoke to a pretty dark-haired woman when I came through a while back," he said. He continued on, describing the few moments he had spoken with my mother. It must have been while I had slept.

"That's our Chevy," I said. My mother's name sounded odd to me, wrong somehow, when he said it.

"I wouldn't have had her old enough for a son your age," Jack said. "I guess I didn't see your dad."

"He's in Lincoln," I said. "He had to work."

"I see," Jack said. "Is she waiting on you?"

"She's taking a nap," I said. "The heights made her sleepy."

"I see," Jack said. "Look, you want to take a spin on my Bridgestone?"

"I don't exactly know how," I said. "I mean, a bigger bike like this. But thank you."

"Hop on behind. I'll whiz you down to the park and back. It's just a few miles. You'll get the feel for it. I'll show you the gears."

The motorcycle thrummed. I looked across the highway and up at the mountains. It was still bright out, the rocks near the road a perfect rose in the late sun. I climbed on. Jack pushed down the foot pegs for me.

"Just put your fingers in my belt loops," he said. "I'll take it easy."

By the time we pulled up to the Garden of the Gods, my grin felt stitched on my face. I hopped off and sat on a stone and took a deep breath. Jack turned the cycle off and watched me.

"First time's a ripper," he said. "You like it?"

"Sure," I said. "Who wouldn't? I like the way it leans in the curves."

"Throttle, brake, clutch." Jack pointed to each. He tapped his boot on the gearshift. "One high, two, three, four low. It's easier than it should be. And there's no reverse to worry over." He laughed. "Wanna try her?"

"Right now?"

"Tomorrow I'll be a day downwind," Jack said. "It's now or not. I'll slide back, and we'll take a spin through the Garden." He stepped off the motorcycle. "Here, hold the machine."

I took the weight of the Bridgestone and then straddled it. Jack watched as I checked the shift and the clutch, clicked up and down through the gears. Then he climbed on behind me.

"I trust you," he said.

All around the asphalt loop he talked in my ear, pointing out the rock formations, but I don't think I saw any of them. I only saw the road unrolling under my feet like the smoothest black rock, felt the motorcycle alive between my legs like a steel bird.

When we came back around to the entry, Jack said I was a born rider. He told me to go ahead and take it on home. I didn't even stop. We were back at the Rock Garden in minutes.

"Wow." I tried to catch my breath. I felt like I'd been running instead of riding. "How fast have you gone on it?" I asked him. We sat down on the wide wooden porch steps.

"I've cranked her past ninety," Jack said. He pulled out a Chesterfield and lit up, then tilted the open pack toward me. "Smoke?"

"I don't," I said. "It's a great machine. Thanks for the ride. Thanks for letting me ride."

"You're fully welcome, son." Jack pulled on his smoke. He took his sunglasses off and looked over his shoulder at the cabin. "I guess you'll remember me now, won't you?"

"I will," I said. "How could I forget?"

The light began to change color. The air was cooler. I thought of my mother for the first time since I sat down on the Bridgestone. I wondered if she'd heard us come up. Jack flicked his smoke away. It landed in the petalled cup of one of the plastic tulips set in gravel by the porch.

"Well, unless you're gonna ask, I guess it's highway time for me."

"Ask what?"

"Once you nibble, you might as well eat the whole hog." He stood and gestured toward the motorcycle and then to the highway.

"You mean what I think?"

"There's more than a half hour of daylight left. You be back before you need the lights. I'll stretch out in one of these log loungers right here."

I thought about what would happen if I wrecked it. How would I pay for it? I didn't think about getting hurt. I couldn't get hurt.

"Just one minute," I said. I stood up.

"The light's going west," Jack said, looking at the sky.

I went up the steps and into my mother's room. It was dim. She still slept on the bed. Her shoes were off now, and the pint bottle stood on the floor by the bed, her glass beside it, the ice melted. She wasn't going anywhere. I turned the lock on the door and pulled it shut.

"OK with Mama?" Jack asked. He held out the key to the motorcycle.

"I just let her know where I was going," I said. I took the key. "Thanks. I'll just drive it up to the Garden again and right back. It won't be long."

"I never had to ask my mama about anything," Jack said.

"What do you mean?" I looked straight into his eyes for the first time. They were such a light blue that it was hard to tell where they were looking.

"Never had one." He laughed.

"I'm sorry," I said. I wanted to get on the bike. I wasn't sure what he was talking about.

"Just a joke," Jack said, laughing again. "Just my kind of joke. Go on now." He tapped the fender of the Bel-Air. "I have collateral here, so don't go running off on me." He held out his hand, and we shook again, the way buyers and sellers do, as if we were closing a deal. Jack sat down on the car hood, his boots on the bumper.

I was running sixty again before I even knew it. I drove to the Garden and followed the easy curves around the same short loop as before, leaning the cycle toward the blue-black asphalt. Rock pillars and boulders loomed above me in the twilight like grand ruins. There was no traffic. I made three loops before I even thought of heading back, and then I went around one more time.

From a long way off I saw a man walking at the side of the highway. He waved me over. It was Jack. I could see the motel in the distance.

"You're pushing the light," Jack said. "I came after you."

"I'm sorry," I said, looking around. The sky wasn't really dark yet. I reached toward the ignition key.

"Leave her run," he said. "I have miles to go." He leaned over the bike and clicked on the headlight. "I love to cover ground after dark."

I stepped off the motorcycle. "Where're you headed next?"

"I never know," he said. He climbed on.

"Thanks again," I said.

Jack was grinning. "I won't mention it!" he yelled as the tires rolled. I watched him roar away and then I turned and walked slowly toward the motel. My mind was washed out from the wind and speed. My eyes were teared up, and I felt weak in my legs.

When I climbed the cabin steps, there was a light on in my mother's room. I knocked on her door, but I heard nothing. I reached in my pocket for the key, but then I saw my door, at the other end of the porch, standing wide open. I went into my room. Both doors to the bathroom were open, mine and my mother's, and the bathroom light was on.

"Mom?" I called out for her as I walked into the bathroom. Something smelled bad, foreign. I glanced in the toilet and then quickly away. I flushed the handle and lunged into my mother's room.

All I could see was her head on the pillow, the bedspread pulled up to her neck. "Mom?" She shifted but didn't open her eyes as I knelt beside her. I froze and watched her breath under the bedspread. Slowly her chest rose and fell and rose again. I folded the bedspread down partway. Her blouse was rumpled, and all but the two bottom buttons were undone. Her hand lay on her chest. I pressed my finger under her wrist, feeling her pulse, straining to tell it from my own. I counted to five, steadily, then ten, fifteen, twenty.

I looked around. On the floor by the bed was the same bottle, but it was empty now. Beside the bottle lay her open purse and wallet. I leaned down and grabbed the wallet. The cash was gone—at least thirty dollars. I couldn't find her pill bottles anywhere.

I stood up and sat right back down. I moved her shoulders, but she didn't stir. I checked her pulse one more time, and then I pulled the bedspread down. Her underwear lay on the sheet next to her. I flipped the cover up again.

I walked to the window. I wanted to punch my fist through one of the panes, as if that could let all the bad things in the room rush out and disappear in the mountains. I thought about the phone in the motel office, the old lady manager, the police. I tried to imagine them in this room with my mother and me. It was almost entirely dark now. I imagined the headlight of the Bridgestone, piercing through the night somewhere miles away.

NINE TEN AGAIN

I didn't break the window. I turned from it and went back over to the bed. I picked up my mother's wallet again and unfolded the cash from my shirt pocket and put it in her wallet and put her wallet back in her purse. Then I went into the bathroom and dampened a washrag and unfolded a towel. I washed my face and hands, several times, splashing hot water into my eyes, over and over again, until I was sure I was ready to drive.

~

We passed North Platte, the halfway point, about dawn. As the sun rose in my eyes, I glimpsed ribbons of sunlit water wandering through sandbars and willow, the strands of the wide Platte River. In the shallow water long-necked birds stood motionless on thin legs, as if they'd been there all night, or forever.

My mother had woken up only once since we had been on the road, right before we crossed back into Nebraska. She was groggy and thirsty and didn't know where we were. I gave her water out of the bourbon bottle I'd rinsed out and filled up at the motel. She went right back to sleep.

Watching the Platte appear and disappear now, I fiddled with the radio, the volume turned low. None of the music seemed right, and the news was all about civil rights and the President and his high-cultured wife. I spun the dial slowly through two church services before I even realized it was Sunday. Near the low end of the dial I heard words in a foreign language, a little like German, but not German, stranger even than German. Then the same voice spoke in English, announcing the station: KRCB, broadcasting Sunday services from the Rosebud Reservation in South Dakota. I looked out the window. Far to the north of the Platte, green hills rolled away toward the Dakotas. The strange language came back on. I turned the radio off.

My mother stretched her legs and rolled toward the

window. I had had trouble getting her into the car. She had mumbled something while I carried her, but the only thing I could make out was my name. Or my father's. I didn't know which.

I steered back onto the Interstate again. It was open in long alternating sections all across the state, but not quite finished and hooked together yet. There were cars ahead of me and cars behind, and cars in the west lanes, going where I was leaving. The traffic was so neatly divided, moving in opposite directions, yet the people in the cars were all going toward their little private futures, whether east or west.

The sun rose higher. I opened my window and flipped the visor down. Ahead of me a hawk circled a field littered with clods and the stalks of disked-in weeds. Two semi-trailers roared by in the westbound lanes, almost neck and neck, pushing through that side of the morning. Pain and evil were loose in the world. There was no point in trying to tell them apart.

My mother stirred again. "Cane?"

She raised her hand into blank air and let it fall onto the seat. Her eyes opened, squinting into the sun. I pulled her visor down and looked over at her, as ready as I would be. But I didn't need to be ready. We didn't speak of it then, or later, or ever, finally.

I couldn't even tell if she saw me. She squinted in my direction, too, as if my face was too bright to look at, and closed her eyes again. That was fine with me. I didn't want her to wake up now. I didn't want her to wake up at least until we were home.

I cranked the window back up. The rush of wind in my ears stopped in a heartbeat—a loud faucet shut down. It was very quiet.

My mother's given name was Valerie. I put my hand on top of hers and kept driving.

Phil Condon's previous books are *Montana Surround* (essays), *River Street* (stories), and *Clay Center*, a novel award recipient from the New Orleans Faulkner Society. He has received an NEA Creative Writing Fellowship and his work has appeared in *The Georgia Review*, *Shenandoah*, *Epoch*, *Prairie Schooner*, *Manoa*, and many other journals. He teaches Environmental Writing and Literature in the Environmental Studies Program at the University of Montana in Missoula.

POETRY TITLES FROM ELIXIR PRESS

Circassian Girl by Michelle Mitchell-Foust
Imago Mundi by Michelle Mitchell-Foust
Distance From Birth by Tracy Philpot
Original White Animals by Tracy Philpot
Flow Blue by Sarah Kennedy
A Witch's Dictionary by Sarah Kennedy
Monster Zero by Jay Snodgrass
Drag by Duriel E. Harris
Running the Voodoo Down by Jim McGarrah
Assignation at Vanishing Point by Jane Satterfield
The Jewish Fake Book by Sima Rabinowitz
Recital by Samn Stockwell
Murder Ballads by Jake Adam York
Floating Girl (Angel of War) by Robert Randolph
Puritan Spectacle by Robert Strong
Keeping the Tigers Behind Us by Glenn J. Freeman
Bonneville by Jenny Mueller
Cities of Flesh and the Dead by Diann Blakely
The Halo Rule by Teresa Leo
Perpetual Care by Katie Cappello

FICTION TITLES

How Things Break by Kerala Goodkin

LIMITED EDITION CHAPBOOKS

Juju by Judy Moffat
Grass by Sean Aden Lovelace
X-testaments by Karen Zealand
Rapture by Sarah Kennedy
Green Ink Wings by Sherre Myers
Orange Reminds You Of Listening by Kristin Abraham
In What I Have Done & What I Have Failed To Do
   by Joseph P. Wood
Hymn of Ash by George Looney
Bray by Paul Gibbons